STORMY NIGHT
AGNES TAYLOR MYSTERY
Book 4

EVA BERNHARD

EB Press

ISBN 978-1-0690966-7-8 (eBook)

ISBN 978-1-0690966-8-5 (Standard Font Paperback)

ISBN 978-1-997787-10-5 (Standard Font Hardcover)

ISBN 978-1-0690966-5-4 (Large Print Paperback)

ISBN 978-1-0690966-6-1 (Large Print Hardcover)

Editorial Services by Pam Clinton at pccProofreading

Cover design by EB Press with a Microsoft Designer AI generated cover image. Background image courtesy of Guru Muxamil under license from Prexels.

This is a work of fiction. All the names, characters, businesses, institutions, places, events and incidents in this book are either the product of the author's imagination or used in a fictitious manner. Any resemblance to actual persons, living or dead, or actual events is purely coincidental and unintended.

 Formatted with Vellum

Books by Eva Bernhard

Agnes Taylor Mystery Series

Absent Beauty - Short Read Prequel

Silent Sands — Book 1

Writer's Death — Book 2

Snowbound — A Holiday Mystery — Book 3

Stormy Night — Book 4

Louise Penfold Mystery Series

Death at Rosewood Manor — Book 1

Death at Eagle Roost — Book 2

EB Press Release

BREAKING NEWS

LOUISE PENFOLD MYSTERIES

DEATH AT ROSEWOOD MANOR

CASCADE GAZETTE — SPECIAL REPORT

A condolence card delivered before its time has unsettled new resident Louise Penfold. Locals say the freelance editor, recently moved from the city, has uncovered troubling circumstances around the recent death of a well-known Cascade resident.

Authorities remain tight-lipped, but whispers suggest secrets at Rosewood Manor may prove darker than its fresh paint.

DEATH AT EAGLE ROOST

HURON DAILY CHRONICLE

Thanksgiving festivities at the lakeside estate Eagle Roost turned tense when visiting editor Louise Penfold and companion Nora Norton encountered a household rife with quarrels.

Sources describe strained relations among guests and hosts. Penfold, already linked to past investigations, is said to be watching closely as unease grows by the hour.

MORE INFORMATION AT AMAZON.COM/DP/B0FR9TDN2T?

For my family and my kind readers whose support means the world to me.
Thank You!

Chapter 1

The oppressive silence spoke louder than the gathering storm. Agnes Taylor shifted uneasily in the afternoon's gloom. Her eyes traveled over the three living room windows. Dense foliage crowded outside the panes, allowing hardly any of the waning light to penetrate. Like tentacles, branches stretched to swipe their sodden leaves across the glass with every gust of wind as if to demand entry.

"Mind if I switch on some lights?" Agnes asked the only other occupant of the room.

"Of course, dear. Go right ahead." Theresa Mae's triple chins wobbled as her homely face looked up from the snaking wool concoction in her lap. "When I knit, I forget all about lights. Could do it in my sleep without dropping a stitch." With a throaty chuckle, she looped wool over her needles.

Yet, Agnes felt the older woman's intense gaze belied the lighthearted words.

"You're not afraid, dear, are you?" Theresa asked.

"Oh, no," Agnes assured her, feeling no such confidence. To prove her nonchalance, she stretched, hands lifting her heavy dark hair as if to twist it into a bun. "Nothing to worry, is there? The house seems very solid."

1

"That it is," said Theresa with conviction. "It weathered Juan and Dorian alright." Another chuckle accompanied her words. She gently poked her graying perm with a knitting needle.

"Oh, were you already here when Dorian hit?" Agnes asked, relieved that her hostess had prior experience.

"No, dear. I moved here a bit later," Theresa said almost regretfully. "Bet your mom never mentioned fall's hurricane season out east. Mind you, officially, it starts in June, but we get the brunt of it in autumn."

"Mom reminded me to pack all my warm stuff for my stint on Prince Edward Island. Said it's no different from anywhere along the North Atlantic coast. The wind chill factor is much worse than back home in Ontario."

In the past, Agnes had been a fair-weather friend of PEI, harking back to a childhood summer. She still recalled her first sight of the red cliffs at Cavendish. They'd toured the home of Anne of Green Gables. A memorable thrill for her as a little girl.

Speaking of her mom Sera made Agnes grab her phone from the round table next to her easy chair. She almost knocked over some bric-à-brac that littered most available surfaces in Theresa's spacious living room.

"Should text Mom to see how they're making out in Halifax," she muttered over Theresa's sounds of agreement. The hurricane threat aborted earlier plans of a cozy mother-daughter weekend after a conference on 19th-century philosophy Agnes attended at a university in New Brunswick. Her mom, Sera, suggested Agnes ought to return straight to PEI to be with Theresa, rather than risk being caught in the storm on a drive southward to Nova Scotia.

Agnes's own gut reaction to the hurricane plowing its way up the North Atlantic had been to point the car due north and escape to Quebec or Ontario if need be. She'd resisted the impulse to turn tail. After all, Sera was the one who'd arranged for Agnes to board at Theresa Mae's B&B while teaching at a PEI college for the fall term. Though Agnes had never met or even hear about Theresa until she came to stay here, helping her mom's friend weather the storm felt right.

Nestled in the Gulf of St. Lawrence, facing the Canadian provinces of Nova Scotia and New Brunswick that were connected by a narrow sliver of land, the Island, as the inhabitants called their water-locked province, seemed rather vulnerable to a storm attack. Windy at the best of times, the Confederation Bridge that spanned eight miles across the Northumberland Straight was a precarious lifeline to the outside world.

Duty bound, Agnes had returned from New Brunswick a few hours ago around midday.

"Sera's quite right," Theresa said while Agnes thumbed her phone. "Mostly, we get south-westerly winds, straight from the US along the Maine coast into the Bay of Fundy. If it's a northerly, it hits us first."

When Agnes nodded, a little distracted, her hostess added, "Give my love to Sera and tell her to stay safe. I'll call her once the storm's over."

"Will do," mumbled Agnes, intent on texting. Theresa Mae and her mom apparently had met years ago. Though Theresa was 20 years younger than Sera's mid-70s, they'd kept loosely in touch. From bits and pieces Agnes had gathered, her hostess bought the B&B three years ago and still had lots of improvement plans.

For Agnes's four-month stint teaching philosophy at a community college, it proved a 'too good to be refused' accommodation despite the 30-minute drive to campus. Though rather isolated for her urban taste, with few neighbors and set several hundred yards back from the highway on forested acreage, the partially renovated house was charming. A lovely room with an ensuite bath at a ridiculously low rate for friendship's sake, combined with being spoiled rotten food-wise, was Agnes's idea of heaven.

Theresa Mae, short in height but generous in width, was fond of indulging in her culinary labors. Hardcore foodie Agnes never passed up a chance to prove herself a competent taster.

Inching farther from the mid-30s point of no return, Agnes often worried where her passion for food, joined at the hip with a sedate academic lifestyle, would lead her. Put a plate of freshly baked double chocolate chip cookies in front of her and worries dissolved faster than the chips could melt.

The ping of her mother's reply ripped Agnes out of her chocolaty musings and made her sit up.

"Mom says the hurricane made landfall. They say it's bad." She glanced at Theresa, who placidly fed the yarn to her knitting needles. "Should we turn on the news?" Neither her hostess nor she were fans of TV and its relentless advertisements. Yet, a hurricane watch warranted an exception.

"I'd rather not, dear. All news about nasty politics and criminals. Heard an alert about drugs. Some stuff with a funny name. Drug crisis on the Island? I ask you, what next?"

"Sounds unlikely," Agnes said, only half listening.

"Did you hear of the hold-up just today? Cashier shot! Here on PEI. What's the world coming to?" The older woman clucked her tongue in tact with her knitting needles.

When Agnes murmured, "Oh? Where was that?" Theresa was already back to the weather. "No use getting all worked up, Agnes. By the time it's here, the storm might've run out of steam, and we'd be biting our nails for nothing."

As if to prove Theresa wrong, branches tapped the windows, propelled by a vicious gust.

"Better close the curtains and lock this nasty weather out," said her hostess and rested her needles, ready to get up.

"Stay put, Theresa. I'll draw them and switch on the light." Agnes looped her long black-brown hair behind her ears and unfolded her jeans-clad legs. As she rose, she shivered. Aware of a chill in the room, she tucked the fleece sweater closer around her body. The house was drafty and could do with energy-efficient windows. Probably one of the countless items on her hostess's bucket list.

Theresa had turned most of the main floor into a huge, yet inviting, open space. A large sofa facing the living room and a giant antique harvest table for informal meals on the kitchen side made for a functional division. Various armchairs, settees, and rocking chairs with side tables built comfortable islands for guests to congregate.

Agnes had barely shut out the weather and turned on a few table and floor lamps when she heard a clattering noise. It came from the front foyer, leading off the generous open-concept space.

"That'll be Dougie," commented Theresa.

"Oh?" Agnes hadn't realized there was another guest. She'd seen no sign of anyone else staying at the B&B when she arrived back from the conference after a four-day absence.

"Dougie, is that you?" called her hostess.

The man who entered wasn't what the appellation had conjured up in Agnes's mind. For one, he was much too old for the diminutive of what presumably was a Douglas. No taller than her own 5'6", he appeared a prim and proper bespectacled chap in his mid-50s, same age as their hostess. Did Theresa know him from boyhood and hence, the nickname?

He must have shed his outerwear in the entrance foyer and now stood in a gray suit with a white shirt and nondescript tie showing above its lapels, rubbing his pink hands either from cold or habit.

"Good day, good day, ladies," he said heartily and approached as if unsure of his welcome.

"Goodness, am I ever glad you got home alright. Bet the drive back was none too pleasant." Half out of her chair already, Theresa clucked her tongue. "Poor man. You must be needing a nice strong tea."

"Thank you kindly, but that's quite all right, my dear lady. Don't disturb yourself on my account. I had a large coffee to keep me company on the drive from Charlottetown."

His feeble voice fit his appearance, thought Agnes, as the man stroked his thinning, mousy hair over a bald spot on his cranium and eyed her questioningly.

While Theresa sank back into her chair, Agnes moved a little closer, ready to introduce herself when her hostess beat her to it.

"Dougie, this is Agnes Taylor, I told you about. She's the daughter of my dear friend, Sera."

"Ah," he said. "So pleased to meet a real philosophy professor. Our good landlady told me all about you." To Agnes's dismay, the proffered hand was cold and damply soft. It felt like a dead flounder.

"Oh, I sure hope not, Mr. ... um." Agnes stalled and suppressed an urge to wipe her hand on her jeans. No way she'd call the man Dougie.

An unexpected glint in his eyes told her he was aware why she hesitated, but his voice betrayed no irony. "Douglas Junior, at your service." He actually bowed, which his hairdo took amiss and came undone. Longer strands covering the pate fell forward onto his brow, only to be swept back into place.

"Eh? Pardon me. Junior, what?" She replied, somewhat frazzled by the display.

A squeaky little laugh parted the narrow lips over brilliantly white small teeth. "Gotcha! Junior is the last name. Fairly uncommon, I grant you. But there it is. Blame it on my ancestors. Just Dug with 'u' is fine."

"Well, Taylor is more common," Agnes said, though she wasn't about to tell him that her mom had their last name anglicized when they first came to Canada.

"Dougie's a family man," Theresa said fondly. She'd been following their interchange with an expression almost of motherly pride. "Would you believe it, Agnes? The good man has five kiddies at home. Doesn't look it, does he?"

While Agnes wondered what five children would do to a man's exterior, though she could well imagine it to wreak havoc with her own figure, Theresa asked Doug, "How's your wife? She must be some worried what with the hurricane and you far from home." In an aside to Agnes, she confided, "Dougie's family lives in Winnipeg. Isn't that so?"

"That's right," he confirmed. "Wife and kiddies are just dandy, last thing I heard. Counting on Daddy being home for Christmas. With a sack full of presents like a good little Santa," he added with a wry smile.

Agnes couldn't make him out. Underneath the veneer of dapper, if somewhat caricatural family man, lurked a deeply satirical streak as if he were playing his part only too well.

At his sudden, penetrating gaze she mustered a conventional smile.

Her impression was deepened when he said, "Now I leave you

good ladies to your little chat and handicrafts, and Dougie will mosey on to do his homework." With a jaunty wave and a cheerio, he toddled to the staircase. On his way, he stopped to straighten a seascape painting that was the slightest bit askew. Apparently satisfied, he mounted the stairs to the upper floor.

Watching his departure, Agnes couldn't suppress an incredulous smirk. Her hostess appeared to find the man's antics quite normal. Was Theresa sweet on this guy? A father of five? Surely not. Yet a gaggle of youngsters might trigger her motherly instincts.

With a slight groan, the object of Agnes's reflections struggled from the depth of the plushy armchair onto stocky legs.

"Better have a last peek at my hens. I can't shake this feeling there's a latch left undone," Theresa said, shaking her head as if in self-doubt.

"What? Now? But the storm."

"You stay high and dry, dear. I'll be back in a jiffy. I'd never forgive myself if something happened to my cluckers. The storm's bound to ruffle their feathers."

The good-natured laugh made Agnes wonder if the hens were of more importance than their owner's safety. Still, there were no two ways about it. "Wait up, Theresa. I'll come with you."

Moments later, they stood swaddled in stiff, yellow raincoats and rubber boots that Theresa kept handy at the entrance, Agnes's pair two sizes too large for her feet.

"Ready?" asked Theresa, one hand on the door handle, the other bracing the door that opened toward the inside.

"Right. Let's do it," said Agnes.

As soon as the door opened, a gust of wind hit them, spewing raindrops into their faces and yanking at their hoods. Agnes grabbed the door with both hands and pulled it shut behind them. Out on the raised wrap-around porch, soggy leaves and plant debris raced along the wooden planks like an army in panicky retreat.

"Wow," she yelled over the roar, "that was fast. Thought it would take hours for the storm to get here."

"Hard to predict a whirlwind," said Theresa, grabbing her arm and leaning close. "It's not the real hurricane. Bet it'll get much stronger."

They struggled against the gusts that hit them sideways when they clambered down the porch stairs and around the building's corner to the shed housing Theresa's favorite brood.

The various flaps, or whatever the openings were called, appeared securely latched to Agnes. So was the door into the shed. Still, Theresa went around examining each while angry gusts flapped their yellow slickers.

"I'll do a quick check around," Agnes called to Theresa.

Upon her return today, they'd moved outdoor furniture, barbeque, portable planters, and anything the two of them could carry to the old barn across from the backyard. Heavier stuff they'd secured with ratchet straps and ropes.

One thing they couldn't do anything about was the tall trees crowding in on the house. A glance up into the gloomy canopies, whipping back and forth with every gust, made Agnes's heart race at the thought of one of these giants snapping and crashing onto the roof. Were the bedrooms upstairs safe during a hurricane?

"All safe here," came Theresa's voice from behind. "Let's run back in before the deluge." She held up a pink palm as if to test the fat drops spattering them now with a vengeance.

As she turned into the wind, Agnes's hood flapped back. Her long tresses beat against her cheeks. One hand twirling her hair into a damp bun, she pulled the hood up and held onto it with a clenched fist.

When they rounded the house to the porch stairs, Theresa stopped in her tracks, making Agnes almost bump into her chubby back.

"Well, that's one for the books," the older woman said over Agnes's "Sorry."

Then Agnes saw what Theresa pointed at. A dark-colored SUV pulled up next to the wooden stairs leading to the wide entrance porch.

As they hurried closer, Theresa's arms stretched out as if to enfold the newcomers from afar. The driver climbed out while the passenger remained hunched over in the front seat on the vehicle's off-side.

A wide-hooded black rain jacket shrouded the driver's face, and its XXL size hid much of the tall figure. Still, Agnes thought, the momentary hip swing suggested a woman rather than a man.

Her surmise proved correct when the newcomer's contralto voice shouted a hearty hello over the rising storm.

"Surprise, surprise. We're back!"

Chapter 2

Moments later, they were crowding in the foyer, struggling out of wet coats and footwear and hampered by the newcomers' backpacks and bulky duffle bag.

An odd couple the arrivals seemed on closer inspection. The tight space exaggerated the female's physique. Her ultra-short hair emphasized the bullish neck and well-padded shoulders.

Unwrapped, the tall woman's companion proved a puny guy with a weaselly face and red-rimmed eyes and nose. To Agnes, he looked about her first-year students' age, several years younger than the woman's early twenties. His nervous fingers pulled the strings of his midnight-blue hoody so tight its hood hugged and distorted his pinched features.

The short run from the vehicle into the house could hardly have chilled him to the bone, Agnes thought. Yet, his body seemed aquiver. Hope he's not ill, she thought. And spreads germs, to judge by the runny nose, her mind commented. Most likely, he indulged in cannabis, she deduced as her own nose twitched in distaste at the odor emanating when he passed her.

"Come in. Make yourself at home." Theresa urged them to move on into the open kitchen area and addressed the woman. "Grab a chair, Carmen, and tell me what brought you and Leo back so soon. I'll put on the kettle. Or how about some nice, mulled cider?"

Though their hostess had introduced the young woman outside, Agnes didn't recall her mentioning the guy's name before. Was he used to being overlooked next to his towering and forceful girlfriend, if that's what she was? Or did his personality predispose him to withdraw into himself? Either way, he paid no heed to Theresa's question. Nor did he meet anyone's eye when he hunched down on the closest chair at the broad harvest table.

Both Agnes and Carmen voted enthusiastically for hot cider.

While Theresa bustled to collect ingredients for the brew, she instructed Agnes to fetch a fruitcake from the pantry. As if quite at home, Carmen reached for mugs and plates in the natural wood cabinets that lent the kitchen such a welcoming atmosphere.

"Mind you, I'm that glad to see you again, Carmen dear," Agnes heard Theresa say and then add quickly with faked warmth, "You too, Leo. There, I thought you well on your way home."

Carmen's sonorous chuckle matched her voice. "Oh man, did we ever try to get out of here. Before the storm, I mean. No luck. Got stuck with trees blocking the road. Didn't we, Leo?"

Why would she ask her mate to verify her words? Agnes wondered. The guy, curled on a chair at the scrubbed pine table as if trying to roll himself into a ball, merely grunted to his navel.

Apparently, that served as a sufficient confirmation of the tale's veracity, for Carmen went on, "Took us ages to get to Borden and, bloody hell, wasn't that damn bridge closed down?" Carmen threw up her large hands and laughed. "Pardon my French. But really, what a bummer. So, here we are back like bad pennies."

Clucking not unlike her hens, Theresa empathized, "Tough luck, you poor dears. And you leaving at the crack of dawn to get out of this nasty weather. Mind you, driving all the way to Ontario in a day? A bit much, isn't it?"

"Nah, no big deal with two driving. Under 17 hours, Google says."

Yeah, right, Agnes thought. Google estimates would change with every traffic jam and construction along the thousand-plus miles ride.

"You can't outrun a hurricane, is what I say," said their hostess. "Bet you'd have gotten stuck somewhere up in New Brunswick with no nice B&B in sight if you'd made it across the bridge."

The renewed mention of the bridge brought Agnes's mind to a stuttering halt. Confederation Bridge closed?

Then, the implications hit her full force. With that connection to the mainland cut off, and obviously the only ferry service to Nova Scotia farther down the Northumberland Straight shut down in storms, the only way out was by air or sea. No option during a hurricane. She'd already seen some fishing boats towed by trailers when she came back today. Probably the stragglers. Most would have hauled their boats out of the water the day before.

Her mind reeled at the realization of what amounted to an island-wide lockdown.

"Then we are trapped," she blurted out.

"Eh? What? What?" The squeal drew everyone's attention to the guy, whose bloodshot eyes stared panicky at Agnes.

"Leo!" boomed Carmen, shooting him a ferocious glance.

He shrank back into himself, the hood shrouding his features as if to cover his being shamed.

Poor guy, thought Agnes, as she apologized for startling him. Aware of the Greek derivation of his name, *leōn* for lion, it seemed a sad irony to be called Leo when fearful as a mouse. Can't have an easy time of it with a dominant partner.

"Hush, dear. Don't get into a tizzy." Theresa, who'd been bustling to and fro from stove to fridge and sundry cabinets, now stood wooden spoon in hand and favored them with a tight smile. "Cider's ready. Agnes, cut us some cake."

When she passed by Leo to grab the knife Theresa proffered, the reek of cannabis permeated the air around him. Perhaps he was spaced out much of the time, anyway, she figured, and opted for a seat at the other end of the long table.

He touched neither food nor drink as the women settled to enjoy their snack. The cinnamon and clove aroma of the still simmering cider filled the kitchen and did much to soothe them.

By way of conversation, Agnes asked Carmen, "How come you

drove all the way back when you were already at the bridge in Borden?" A good 45-minute drive under normal weather conditions, it seemed an odd choice to return to this B&B in rural PEI.

Carmen pointed a forefinger to her mouth and kept on chewing sticky fruitcake.

"Bet there wasn't a vacancy for miles around Borden. Happens every time the bridge shuts down," explained Theresa.

After a gulp from her mug and an exaggerated swallow, Carmen reached out a hand to their hostess and responded sweetly, "We hated to think of you all alone in the storm. Didn't we, Leo?" she added with a sideways glance at the morose figure.

Perhaps still ticked off by the admonition, the young man muttered something under his breath, not meeting anyone's eye.

To Agnes's mind, he didn't appear the type to give a hoot if a chance acquaintance must ride out a hurricane by her lonesome.

What stereotype! Agnes's better self promptly harangued her with a homily. The guy might have a caring nature. Who are you to make snap judgments? You, of all people, with your track record of misjudging the males of the species.

Suitably rebuked by her moral monitor, Agnes seconded Theresa's warm thanks for the young couple's thoughtfulness. Strange, though. The older woman failed to mention there was no danger of loneliness with Agnes and Doug in the house. Funny, that man hadn't made an appearance yet. If he was in a room to the back upstairs, he might not hear them.

"Well, I'd better boil water and fill my thermoses," announced Theresa, heaving herself up. "Power's bound to go off any moment," she added when the energy-saving candle bulbs of the wrought iron chandelier above the table flickered. "No power, no well pump."

With a sigh, she waddled to the sink, filled a large electric kettle, and busied herself lining up insulated jugs of various sizes.

"We've got flashlights," Carmen said. She reached into a backpack slung over the chair's backrest. The fat, rubberized torch she unearthed was huge, like everything about the woman. She switched it on and waved the thing as if warding off the stormy night. "But I want to have a bath before the light goes. Can nap in the dark after."

She guffawed. "We take the big room with the ensuite. We can swing it for one night, can't we, Leo?"

As expected, no reply beyond a sniff came from that quarter. The man was still engaged in contemplating his navel. Figuratively speaking. What a pair. Made one wonder if romance was all it was cracked up to be, thought Agnes with a grin. Carmen, however, was in for a disappointment.

Theresa set her straight before Agnes could. "Sorry, dear," said Theresa, and padded back to the table, kettle in hand. "Agnes here has the blue room. She's a professor and stays with me until the end of the fall term, just before Christmas. Don't you, honey?" She patted Agnes' shoulder with her free hand.

Turning back to the sulking Carmen, Theresa added, "No chance of a hot bath, I'm real sorry, Carmen. Agnes and me filled the tub this afternoon and a few pails for when the power goes. Need water for the toilets, don't we?"

"You're kidding me," Carmen leaned forward. "You've got to have hot water in a B&B."

"But, dear. We're on a well. And that needs electricity for the pump to run. You must know that? All houses out in the country are on wells." Theresa's apologetic tone did little to soothe the young woman's temper. "No worries, I won't charge you for the night."

The offer did nothing to appease. Carmen rolled her eyes, and her mouth twitched, presumably in distaste at such inconvenience. With a petulant pout, she insisted, "I really wanted that room. We've got the money for one night. Can't you refill the tub after I've had my hot bath? The power's still on."

Not waiting for an answer, she reached out to Agnes across the table. "You don't mind if I use your bathroom. Yours is much nicer than the old one."

Of all the nerve, Agnes thought indignantly. She was spared correcting Carmen's misconception and voicing her 'no way' politely when something banged against the center window in the living room behind them.

It made skinny Leo almost jump out of his hoodie. As the hood flapped back with the guy's violent spasm, Agnes glimpsed red-veined eyeballs, the gray irises rolled up to be next to invisible. The eerie sight made her shiver.

"Hell, it's only the wind," Carmen told him but leaned in to squeeze his bony shoulder. Her smile seemed forced when she told Agnes, "Leo has astraphobia." She pronounced it carefully and added, "Fear of thunderstorms."

"Yeah, I know my Greek. I guess some people fear the noise rather than the visual manifestation." Even while she spoke, Agnes regretted falling into her professorial tone and suppressed an urge to show off her education in Classics. Yet, the young woman irked her.

"Whatever," commented Carmen and turned to Theresa, who'd walked over to the window to check behind the heavy drapery and now came back, muttering, "Should have listened to Joe up the road. You've met him, Agnes. Or maybe not. Boards up all windows of his place. Mind you, it's an old farmstead. Offered to do mine for the hurricane. Just plywood sheets, you know."

"God, no. I'd get claustrophobic being cooped up like that." Agnes shuddered at the idea. "Like being in a coffin."

"Better alive in a coffin than dead in a storm, dear, is what Joe says." Theresa laughed good-naturedly.

"Yikes," cried Agnes. "That's nightmarish. I don't even want to be dead in a coffin."

"How silly." Carmen echoed their hostess's laugh, clearly enjoying the ghoulish theme. "You're usually dead in coffins. Unless they bury you alive. There's no other way."

"I just don't like the idea of supplying food for the worms." Feeling her tone grow defensive, Agnes added reasonably, "I want my ashes thrown to the winds. Free to mingle with the elements, is all."

"Death by fire is the worst." The squeaky cry from the silent visitor stunned them momentarily.

Carmen leaned over and ruffled the guy's hair, or hood, since he'd retreated into its shelter. "Silly goose," Agnes heard her murmur. It sounded quite affectionate.

What a strange relationship. The thought hardly crossed her mind when her moral monitor kicked in. If the roles were reversed and a hunk of a guy would treat his pint-sized partner that way, you'd call him a chauvinist and sexist. There's nothing wrong with a woman being older and tougher than her mate.

A renewed bang cut off her mental chatter. This time, it came from the front door.

"Goodness! We're busy like in July," joked Theresa, pushing herself up from the groaning wooden chair she'd barely sunk into.

"Stay put. I'll get it," Agnes offered and made for the foyer.

Surprised to find Carmen in her wake, Agnes told the woman somewhat curtly, "Thanks. I can manage."

The smile she received in return struck Agnes as condescending. So did Carmen's words.

"You never know who comes calling on a night like this."

Chapter 3

The cramped foyer made it difficult to assert herself, but Agnes wasn't about to let the young woman domineer her. Yet, an exasperated eye roll was wasted on someone who stood at least six or eight inches taller than her own 5'6".

"That's right," came Theresa's hushed comment from the rear. Her graying head peeked around Carmen's broad torso and reached barely to chest height. In a whisper, she added, "Told you about that cashier shot Prince County way. We can't be too careful with all that riffraff nowadays."

As if a B&B were a likely target for armed robbers, Agnes thought. Still, the place was Theresa's, and there was a momentary flicker of something like fear even in Carmen's pale-gray eyes.

Somewhat uncertain, Agnes asked, "Well, are we going to check who's there?"

Theresa rallied already. "We'd better—"

Carmen jostled past Agnes. "Here. Let me." Then, in a lighter tone, "The storm's gonna rip that door right out of your hands. I'm a barbell swinging girl. Used to hold my own." The sonorous chuckle eased the tension.

Agnes bowed to common sense and let the stronger deal with Mother Nature.

A vicious gust barged in as soon as Carmen eased the door open a mere foot wide. Soggy leaves swirled into the entranceway.

Theresa's arm reached past Agnes to flip a switch. In the yellow beam of the porch lantern, Agnes could make out a dark shape that moved into the light. Another, shorter one, brought up the rear.

"We're closed," Carmen informed them without as much as a glance at Theresa.

Their hostess wasn't standing for such highhandedness. With an "Excuse me" to Agnes, she squeezed past to the door that Carmen was about to shut.

"Thank you, Carmen," she said firmly, and stepped into the gap, ignoring the rain spattering her. "I'll take it from here."

Carmen had no choice but to retreat behind the door and prevent it from flinging wide open.

Over Theresa's head, Agnes could now see two rain-drenched men on the porch. The taller had to shout over the roaring storm. "Can we come in, please? Damn truck broke down half-a-mile back. Saw your B&B sign."

"Do you have ID and can—"

An ear-splitting crack of splintering wood drowned Theresa's last words. With one hand on her heart, her other hand gesticulated wildly, beckoning the men to enter. Once they were safely inside, Agnes and Theresa retreated into the kitchen to make room. Theresa said, "Not safe for you standing out there."

Carmen banged the door shut and pivoted to stand wide-legged with her back to it. Brows contracting, she eyed the males suspiciously.

Their hostess's maternal instincts apparently overrode concerns. "Take off your wet stuff. Put the boots on the tray there. Agnes, grab some towels from the linen closet. These poor men are soaked to the bone. Carmen? Put on the kettle. Hot tea will warm you up."

"If you add a shot of brandy," Agnes heard the second guy say in a pleasantly jokey tone as she headed for the closet in Theresa's private quarters. She noticed Leo still hunched forward but now with both arms hugging his head as if the noise made it ache.

When she returned a few minutes later, the men stood like drenched poodles by the foyer entrance. Torn between feeling sorry for them and unease about the sudden intrusion, Agnes eyed them closely. Seemed polite enough, she thought, as they mumbled their thanks while rubbing their heads and faces with the fluffy towels she'd handed out.

"Your clothes are all wet," said Theresa, who regarded them with motherly concern. "We'll fix that. Find you something dry."

"Thanks, ma'am. No need." The older of the two men pointed behind him. "S'ppose it'll be dry."

Rugged and brawny, even if somewhat bedraggled at present, he didn't look like someone to mess with. Agnes judged him to be her own age. She almost laughed out loud when his shorter and younger buddy dove back to the door and dragged a dripping wet duffle bag into the kitchen.

Catching her eye, he grinned, saying, "Waterproof. Doesn't look it, eh?"

His voice struck Agnes as warm and friendly. A guy of her own height seemed non-threatening.

"Now, let's get you settled." Theresa ushered them farther into the kitchen. "You can change in the downstairs bathroom and hand me the wet stuff for the dryer. No time to lose, what with that nasty wind picking up. The power's bound to go."

"I don't want to butt in," said Carmen, who stood erect and wide-legged in front of the kitchen counter like an alpha male. "But shouldn't you check their IDs before taking them in? They haven't even given you their names."

"The name's Kieran," said the tall guy, frowning at giant Carmen, who had a good inch or two on him. With a polite smile at Theresa and Agnes, he went on, "That's my cousin, Rob. McGuinty's the family name."

The short McGuinty nodded along but was already busy divesting himself of his wet sweater, and a moment later stood in an equally wet black T-shirt that emphasized how skinny he was. Much like Leo, thought Agnes. Whereas Leo's facial skin appeared grayish, Rob's had the golden tinge of a fading tan. He

looked past his mid-twenties, sinuous and fit rather than emaciated.

Her gaze strayed between the two. Odd. Leo hadn't said a word. There was something furtive and wary about the darting glances Leo shot the newcomers from below the hood he'd pulled tight again to cover much of his own face. Agnes assumed, like some students she'd taught over the years, he must suffer from severe social anxiety or a similar condition.

Unlike Leo, Rob spoke for himself with marked confidence. He took a step toward their hostess, who held out her hand for the discarded sweater. Rather than handing it over, the young man took another quick swipe at his face with the towel, tucked the soaked sweater under his arm, and rubbed his hands dry.

"It's real kind of you, ma'am, to take us drowned rats in," he said and proffered his right hand in greeting. "If you show where it goes, I'll stuff it all into the dryer. It's too icky for you." He smiled an apology.

"I'm used to worse." Theresa chuckled. "You can't be too particular when you run an inn. Lucky, I lost my sense of smell. The things you see... Well, never mind that."

Towel slung over his shoulder, Rob's fingers dug into his back pockets. "You want our— Sh— Left my wallet in the truck, man." He whirled around to his cousin. "Got yours, Kieran?"

His hulk of a cousin grunted and went back into the foyer. Agnes could see him rifle the pockets of a jacket on the coat hooks. He returned, shaking his head. "Shoot. Just pray no one breaks into the truck tonight."

Theresa clucked her tongue in commiseration. But Agnes caught Carmen roll her eyes and mutter, "Yeah, right."

"C'mon. No chance in hell." Rob dismissed his cousin's worry. "Smart folks hunker down. It's only crazy people like us on the go."

"So neither of you has an ID." Carmen's tone cut like a razor. "Pretty odd, if you ask me."

"Didn't hear no one ask you. Eh, Rob?"

Kieran's curt rejoinder astonished Agnes, no matter how right he was. The man seemed to have taken an instant dislike to Carmen.

To Theresa, he spoke quite civilly. "I'm right sorry, ma'am. Got out of the truck real quick."

"Kieran and me would have tried to fix the old pickup," said Rob. "But a tree crashed down right behind it. We grabbed our bag and hoofed it."

"Goodness gracious!" Their hostess clapped a hand over her wide mouth. "How scary for you. Now, don't you worry about a thing."

A slight unease crept into Agnes's mind. Still, innkeepers, especially those of B&Bs, knew next to nothing about the people from far and wide they accommodated. An ID was little reassurance after all. Criminals could easily get a faked one, she surmised.

"You can call our Uncle Ed up Tignish way," Kieran told Theresa.

"We fixed up his place for the storm," Rob chipped in. "He's in his eighties and lives all by himself, now."

Chins aquiver, Theresa praised their enterprise. "That was mighty nice of you. Where's home then?"

"Over Montague way," said Kieran.

"Here. Got a piece of paper? I'll give you Uncle Ed's number, ma'am," volunteered Rob. "We really should have left this morning, but Uncle didn't stock up. Had to get him food and stuff. Figured we'd still beat the storm."

Even her vague sense of island geography told Agnes they'd planned to drive east almost from tip to tip. Not that any trip on PEI took all that long. In good weather, that is.

Their hostess seemed entirely satisfied and ambled over to a phone desk built into the kitchen counter and sank onto the padded desk chair. Pad and pen at the ready, she asked, "What's Uncle's number, then? He's a McGuinty, too? I'll give him a buzz on the landline." She patted the vintage rose-colored rotary phone that graced the desk and, like the comfy chair, reminded of more leisurely conversation times.

"882—"

A tremendous crash, followed by a thud and splintering, cut off Rob's dictation and made everyone jump.

Leo's anguished shriek creeped out Agnes more than the ill-boding racket from outside.

"That darn tree," swore Theresa with uncustomary vehemence. She flung the pen onto the desk and pushed herself up, intent on hustling to the front door.

Agnes rushed to intervene. Kieran was faster. "Allow me, ma'am." His broad shoulders blocked the foyer entrance. "Tree stuff is along my line. Too dangerous for folks to mess with."

"We do lawn care and tree maintenance," said Rob, already by his cousin's side. "No way to fix anything tonight, but we need to check if there's danger to the house. It sounded damn close."

Next to Agnes, Carmen bent over Leo, rubbing his back none too gently. Agnes heard her mutter, "Yeah, right. Another likely story."

Why would anyone lay claim to that line of business unless it were true beat Agnes. Carmen seemed determined to find something wrong with the guys. They struck Agnes as outdoorsy types, who might well be arborists and do yard maintenance.

"Bet it's the one right next to the porch," said Theresa to the guys. "Be careful. We don't want you get hurt."

From behind came another voice. "What on earth happened? It sounded like an earthquake. Was anyone hurt, you say?"

Like everyone else, Agnes swiveled to see Douglas Junior descending the stairs. She'd forgotten all about him.

So apparently had Theresa, who now rushed toward her elusive guest. "My God, Dougie! Did you hear that crash? It's the big maple out front. I'm sure of it."

Doug's prim and proper appearance had a soothing effect, for the tense atmosphere deflated. Attired in dress pants, white shirt, and tie, his only allowance to casual home wear was an immaculate maroon V-neck cardigan. His hair combed meticulously over his pate, he stood still, pink hands folded at belly height.

Amazed, Agnes watched a transformation in Leo. At the sound of Doug's voice, his head had shot up, and he struggled out from under Carmen's hand that rested on his upper back. Agnes could have sworn Leo's face gained color, and his eyes flickered with interest.

They must have met when they stayed before. After all, Theresa mentioned they'd only left this morning. Perhaps the young guy's insecure nature found the family man reassuring. The itinerant father of five might serve as a great paternal substitute for the hapless Leo.

Carmen, however, regarded the man on the stairs with contempt.

While Rob eyed the newcomer curiously, Kieran seemed impatient at the delay. "Gotta know what's what," he said in Theresa's direction, then turned to Agnes, "Here, miss. Can you help Rob with the door? It'll get the full blast when I go out."

"Call me Agnes. I'll be glad to help." She smiled at Rob and followed the guys into the foyer.

"I'll do it." Carmen crowded into the narrow space. "You'll be no good for a muscle job."

Offended, Agnes faced the brazen young woman. From the corner of her eye, she saw Leo use his freedom from oppression to sidle up to Doug, who now stood at the table watching the scene unfold.

Perhaps being under observation caused her acid tone, but Agnes felt she'd had enough. "Do you mind?" she hissed at Carmen. "I think Rob and I can manage just fine."

Carmen's hoot ceased abruptly with the thunderous crash that shook the floor and walls.

Complete darkness fell.

"There goes the power."

Theresa's placid remark had Agnes giggle in counter-reaction to the fright she'd felt at the shaking floor. Was the house coming down around their ears? She dug her nails into her palms to control her nerves. Through shouts and swearing from Carmen and the cousins, there was no howl from Leo. Maybe Doug's presence serve as a pacifier.

"Got a flashlight, ma'am? She'll need checking out." Kieran's call to Theresa.

The 'she,' Agnes guessed, was whatever slammed down outside.

"Hey, what's-your-name! Hang on to the door. Rob, you help," he added.

Agnes made way for Carmen, whose tall body jostled her in passing, causing Agnes to mumble a reflexive "Sorry" as if it were her fault.

"The big one on a hook by the door. Left side," instructed

Theresa. "I replaced them batteries this afternoon. Should've let Joe take down the darn maple. It's not safe to go out now."

The LED flashlight illuminated the door handle.

"Need be." Kieran's voice was flat. But in the reflected white light, Agnes could see determination in his clenched jaw muscles. "Ready?" He tossed his head at Carmen and Rob.

"What're you waiting for?" Carmen growled. "Get on with it."

From behind Agnes came another beam of light, and she felt Theresa's hand on her arm.

Then, a violent gust of wind hit them as the door opened inward. Carmen and Rob stemmed themselves against it as Kieran slipped through the gap and pushed it shut with a thud once he was outside.

"He'd get all wet again," commented their hostess.

Agnes snorted in suppressing another fit of the giggles.

Rob's "Wasn't dry yet, anyway," was almost too much for her frayed nerves.

"Let's get the candle trays and oil lamp, Agnes," Theresa said, waving her flashlight at the kitchen.

"Can I be of any use?" came Doug's voice from the dark interior.

The beam picked him out still at the foot of the stairs. Not a man of action, thought Agnes as his lids blinked nervously in the beam.

"Oh, my God, Dougie," Theresa cried. "I'm real sorry. And you hoping for a good night's sleep, I bet."

At that, his lips twitched. Perhaps the man had a sense of humor, after all. Yet, his words were dry like Agnes imagined his accounting files to be. "Dear Mrs. Mae, we must contend with the facts. Weather events disrupt the best laid plans."

Are those two for real? Agnes felt stumped and couldn't make them out.

Her eyes followed Theresa's torch beam as it panned along the table and stopped dead.

Across the harvest table, sprawled among a puddle of cider and squashed fruitcake, lay Leo.

Chapter 4

It took all of Agnes's willpower not to scream.

"Bring lights," she said with forced calm to Theresa, who stood frozen, flashlight wavering in her shaking hand. Its beam threw bizarre shadows onto the kitchen ceiling, increasing the horror of the figure sprawled across the harvest table.

Knees wobbling, Agnes rushed to Leo's side. The hoodie covered his head, and she had to lean over the mess of spilled tea and squashed fruitcake to ease it back. At least, his face lay sideways, out of reach of the oozing spill beneath his torso.

Gingerly, she pressed two fingers to his neck in search of a pulse. The skin felt clammy, but below it, she could sense warmth. Unsure if it was her own pulse throbbing in her fingertips, she took a moment to calm herself. Then she felt it. With no medical experience, she couldn't tell if the beat rate was normal but beat it did. Holding her fingers half-an-inch from his mouth and nose, she sensed the faintest stir of air. He was breathing.

As she straightened, her own breath expelled in a deep sigh. Leo was alive. Must've jumped up and passed out from fright at the crash and shaking floors.

The room suddenly was much brighter, relatively speaking, not only from relief but from a vintage oil lamp Theresa deposited at a safe distance on the table.

"He fainted, I think," Agnes whispered.

"Poor mite," said Theresa. "He's a scaredy cat, alright. Bet the old maple scared him to death."

Glad the scare hadn't done quite that, Agnes murmured, "I'd better get Carmen." With the storm's howling so much louder in the tight confines of the foyer, neither Carmen nor Rob would have heard what was going on. "Leo might be prone to faints. She'll know what's best for his medical condition." Most likely, his drug dependence, she wagered. Subtle signs had reminded her of students with drug addictions she'd encountered.

"You do that, dear. I'll make him more comfy."

"Er…Perhaps wait for Carmen. I'll be quick," Agnes said and grabbed the flashlight.

Its beam hit the shadowy figure by the stairs. Douglas Junior hadn't moved. When her glance fell on him, he wrung his hands at belly height in a classic gesture of helplessness.

What a useless fellow in an emergency. Exasperated, she rushed to the capable Carmen.

"What's up?" asked Rob, his ear close to the front door as if he might miss his cousin's knock. A distinct possibility with the storm's roar assaulting the front door like a menacing alien creature.

By a leap of thought, Agnes asked, "Shouldn't he be back?" Immediate worry about Kieran superseded the relief at Leo's mere faint.

"No worries, Agnes. My cousin knows what he's doing. Is everyone alright in there?"

With a quick shake of her head, Agnes turned to Carmen, who leaned against the wall by the door's hinges.

"Takes his sweet time about it," the young woman drawled, her expression utterly bored in the flashlight's shielded beam.

Not to startle her, Agnes aimed for a matter-of-fact tone, saying, "Could you see to Leo, please? His astraphobia made him faint at the crash outside, I think."

Far from anxious, Carmen merely grunted and used her shoulder to push away from the wall support, commenting, "Peed his pants like as not. You stay and help this shrimp here when macho comes back."

"Poor bugger," said Rob as they watched the young woman stomp to the kitchen.

"You'd better go back," he added when Carmen was out of earshot. "I can manage. They need you in there."

"You sure?" He looked capable, but two were better than one.

"Worst-case scenario, that doorknob's gonna smash into the drywall if I let go. Hole's easy to fix." Rob's wry, lopsided grin was infectious.

Her own faded when a slapping sound reached them. "Okay. Just holler if you need a hand," she said and rushed back to Leo.

Her suspicion proved correct. Carmen stood behind Leo's chair, his head now resting against her thighs. None too gently, the woman was slapping the guy's hollow cheeks.

"Are you nuts?" hissed Agnes. "What are you doing to him?"

"Mind your bloody business," growled Carmen. "That's how it's done."

"I'm sure there are better ways—"

"A drop of brandy," interrupted Theresa from across the table. "My dear mother always said brandy's a cure-all. I'll get it." She waddled over to a kitchen cabinet.

Oh God, thought Agnes. Between the two, they'll kill him yet. Alcohol's the last he needs if he's on drugs.

Aloud, she suggested in a firm tone, "Let's lower him gently to the floor and prop up his legs a bit." And to Doug, who still watched from afar, "Could you grab a blanket and cushions from the sofa, please?"

Next to her, Carmen grumbled, "Whatever," yet followed Agnes's instructions.

They eased Leo onto the blanket Doug had spread out and fastidiously straightened. Relieved, Agnes observed Leo's lids flutter. He seemed to regain consciousness, and the breathing normalized.

Still, she remained crouched beside to ensure his legs didn't slide off the cushions if he moved. His brain needed all the blood and oxygen it could get.

Gosh, what a night, she thought and made another mental note to sign up for the first aid refresher course she kept postponing.

To Carmen, who stood by with arms crossed in evident displeasure, she said, "Would you get some cold water for him, please? Safer than booze."

With a "Whatever," Carmen strode off.

Hunkered down by Leo's side, Agnes sensed Doug hovering behind her. She was about to tell the man to sit down when Leo's twitching lids opened to reveal bloodshot eyes. Irrelevantly, she noticed how deep they set in their sockets. Like a skull's hollows. Or was that a trick of the weak light?

His stare went past her, and his body wriggled, the torso struggling to rise.

"Hang on. Take it slowly," she said in her calmest tone.

Rather than have him roll over, she slid parallel to his head and shoulders and supported him to a slightly elevated position. From that vantage point, she realized Leo's eyes weren't searching for his partner but fixed on Doug, whose brows knitted furiously.

Not good for the patient. Even if Doug resented Leo's paternal fixation, this wasn't the time to react to it. She cleared her throat to get Doug's attention. Her slight headshake was hardly needed, for the man composed his features into a mildly inane expression.

"Er... Doug? Would you be so kind and grab another blanket and a few cushions? We don't want Leo to catch a chill," she said and was relieved to see him withdraw wordlessly.

Her patient, however, craned his neck after his idol, the gaze filled with yearning like a child's that sees his favorite treat withdrawn.

Some weird hero worship, Agnes surmised, as she studied the pale features that looked so vulnerable. His face appeared immature, especially close up and in repose. Still, he might be older, and some hormonal imbalance slowed maturity.

Poor kid must be desperate for approval. And no wonder, she sighed as Carmen returned that moment, pushing a glass in front of Leo's nose.

"Thanks, Carmen." Agnes reached for the glass before water

could spill onto Leo's chest. "Here. Have a sip, Leo." She eased the glass to his lips while her other arm supported him.

"Water's for cattle, my dear mum used to say," muttered Theresa, brandy held aloft. Upon Agnes's gentle headshake, she raised the snifter to her own lips and downed it in two gulps.

A loud whooshing from the foyer announced Kieran's return.

Agnes caught Carmen's eye and jutted her chin toward the entranceway. "Would you mind—"

"Am I your slave or what?" With a scowl and a toss of her head, the tall woman left.

Needn't have bothered because Rob already entered with a dripping and disheveled Kieran in tow.

Theresa's mouth gaped wide at the sight. And well it might. A grin stole to Agnes's lips. For the returning storm warrior resembled a walking tree. Covered from head to toe in shredded leaves and plant debris that clung to his soaking-wet clothes, he introduced a chimeric vibe.

"Sorry about the mess, ma'am," said Rob.

"Never mind. Can't be helped," their hostess replied while her glance strayed to the broom affixed to a tall kitchen cabinet by the entrance.

"Did you check my SUV?" said Carmen. "I want to get out of here first thing tomorrow."

Trust Carmen to have her priorities straight, thought Agnes.

Rob laughed. "Gotta be kiddin'. No one's leaving in a hurry."

With the advantage of superior height, the woman glared down at him. The oil lamp's flickering light bounced flashes off her widening eyes. "And why's that?" she challenged.

"Ah, just a minor thing like a little hurricane." Rob left the implications dangling.

The cousin, who'd scraped greenish-brown vegetation from his face with a towel proffered by Theresa, said in between swipes, "For one thing, there's the tree. Smashed the porch to bits. Flat like a flounder with the big sucker on top. Me, I'm used to climbing trees." Then, with mounting impatience, "Didn't bother checking your motors under all that mess. Go look if you want."

"I knew it," cried Theresa. "That darn old maple." Then she added, placid as ever, "Well, the porch needed replacing. No great loss. My insurance might pay for it."

Agnes suppressed a chuckle at such practical equanimity and saw a similar amusement flash over Doug's features as he handed her cushions and draped a blanket over the prone Leo, who was shivering in spasms.

Leo should be in bed, she mused while propping him up cautiously.

Back in the shadows, Doug ahem-ed before addressing Kieran in his primmest tone. "Excuse me, young fellow. Are you saying our cars are not operational, and this tree bars the exit?"

"How would I know if your friggin' car works?" Kieran shot back. "Dig her out tomorrow and try. As for the exit. Man, don't you get it? The damn tree smashed the porch to smithereens. Blocks the door."

Into the momentary silence greeting Kieran's angry words, broke Leo's piercing howl.

Rising like Lazarus from the dead, he cried, "I want out!"

Chapter 5

Leo's outcry still reverberated in Agnes's ears. She sucked a sharp breath through her teeth, thinking, he yowls enough to wake the dead.

When he let loose, she'd drawn back as far as her arms extended. Now she leaned in, murmuring inanities like, "There, there. It's okay," realizing it was far from all right for him.

Theresa ambled over and dragged a chair close. She sat squarely facing the scaredy cat as she'd dubbed him.

"Now, don't you go all to pieces just like my porch, young man," she said. "Storm's over soon enough, and you'll be on your way home. No need to carry on like this," she added sternly when Leo whimpered into his clenched fist. Agnes could see his teeth gnawing at the pale skin.

Carmen watched, mouth crooked in contempt. As if it were the most natural thing in the world, she asked, "Anyone got some sedatives? We ran out last night."

"Er...Ahem." Agnes cleared her throat. "Is that the right stuff for—"

"Best thing for the poor lamb," Theresa cut in. "Agnes, there's a prescription bottle in my bathroom. Mirror cabinet. Top shelf. Be a dear and get a couple of tablets. Says Seconal on the label."

When Agnes hesitated, Carmen said, "Don't bother. I'll get it."

She'd empty the bottle, Agnes figured, and scrambled to her feet. "No. You'd better see to Leo." Not waiting for an answer, she grabbed the flashlight from the table.

Their hostess remarked, "Bet this youngster needs a nice nap until supper. Carmen, dear, your sweetheart's best off in bed upstairs."

Unless the roof caves in, flitted through Agnes's mind as she sped to the door at the back of the living room marked 'Private.'

She'd only been in Theresa's sanctum once early on during her stay. Other than a bedsit and bathroom, it contained a large laundry with linen cupboards and an ironing area, plus a utility room. A door at the end of the narrow hallway connected to the backstairs and an exit to the outdoors.

Agnes made straight for the bathroom across from Theresa's bedsit. This one hadn't been renovated. Its simplistic single shower stall and linoleum floor looked worn and dated. The mirrored medicine cabinet above the small sink proved crammed with jumbled cosmetics, body care products, and medications.

Did Theresa hang on to stuff left behind by her guests? The thought disturbed Agnes.

She scanned the top shelf and, on her third attempt, lit on a small orange plastic vial. Labeled by a local pharmacy, the Seconal prescription was issued for Theresa Mae a year ago. It was three-quarters full.

Would the pills be past their expiry date now? The label didn't specify. Presumably, drugs had a longer shelf life than perishable goods. But still. Plus, administering prescription drugs nilly willy felt deadly wrong. Yet, if she didn't come back with two tablets, Theresa might hand over the bottle.

With a sigh, Agnes fiddled with the childproof lid and popped two Seconal into a tissue from a doilied box on the toilet tank.

When she got back to the main area, only Doug was left sitting at the harvest table. He seemed immersed in something held at lap height but stuffed it into his pocket and bounced to his feet when she drew level.

Blankets and cushions scattered the floor in heaps where Leo had lain.

"Everyone gone up?" asked Agnes, just to be polite. She couldn't think of what else to say to this odd fellow.

"So they are, Dr. Taylor," he said and raised a glass of water from the table. "I was about to bring this to young Leo."

Pleasantly surprised the man tried to be useful and kind, after all, Agnes said, "You must have made a memorable impression on Leo in your brief acquaintance. You're the only one he's taken a lively interest in. A father figure, maybe?"

When Doug's face darkened in a scowl resembling anger, she felt crestfallen. Perhaps the man's vanity balked at appearing old enough to serve as a paternal substitute to a boy in his late teens.

"Didn't mean to imply," she stumbled into speech and gazed at the untidy heap on the floor in search of soothing words.

"If you found the pills for the lad, would you like me to deliver them with the water?" Though stilted, Doug sounded his timid self again. "It would save you an unnecessary trip."

"Oh, I'll need something from my room anyway," she said. When the eagerness drained from his face, she added quickly, "Er, on second thought, yes, please. I want to straighten things here first."

She passed him the tissue-wrapped tablets and watched him climb the stairs, water glass held out as if anxious to avoid spills on his dress pants.

Amused, she noticed his polished square-toed patent leather Oxfords. No indoor slippers or wooly socks for the dapper man like the rest of them sported.

By some wild association, her brain's synapses produced the image of another natty petit figure. Hercule Poirot. Or maybe it was David Suchet's marvelous rendition of Christie's PI. Doug could neither lay claim to a magnificent moustache nor an egg-shaped pate. In fastidiousness, Mr. Junior equaled the little Belgian detective any day. Like Hercule, he straightened pictures and knick-knacks that stepped out of line. All the while covertly observing others.

Cushions in hand, Agnes stood and chuckled softly. Her imagination was running riot again. Christie's creation certainly was no father, though he referred to himself as Papa Poirot. In Dame Agatha's yarns, the famous detective showed no great liking for women and children.

Still smiling, she distributed her load among the sofa and chairs and sauntered upstairs just as Theresa descended.

"Dinner in an hour, I told everyone," the older woman announced as they drew level on the halfway landing. "Cold, of course. Salads, cold-cuts, and bread."

"Sounds good to me. I'll be down in five minutes to give you a hand."

"That'll be real kind, dear. Carmen promised to help as soon as her sweetheart settles down. He's a handful, isn't he?"

"Sure is," agreed Agnes with a grin. Leo certainly got them all hopping. "I sent the Seconal up with Doug. Was that okay?"

"Goodness, yes. Such a nice man." Her hostess's chubby features beamed. "Well, dear, see you in a bit." With a pat on Agnes's arm, Theresa shuffled on in her pink faux fur slippers.

Once Agnes reached the top of the stairs that opened onto a cozy sitting area, swooshing and clattering announced the storm's wrathful barrage on the curtained bay window.

Despite the threatening tempest, the paisley loveseat in shades of green and rose, flanked by matching chairs, still retained an air of comfort. So did the bookshelf off to one side, packed with mass-market fiction in lurid colors that rubbed shoulders with respectable literature. The muffled racket from outside, however, caused Agnes to glance at the vaulted ceiling. She momentarily closed her eyes, hoping to God no tree would crash through. Unthinkable, the hurricane gaining force and tearing off not only asphalt shingles but the entire roof.

A slight shiver ran along her arms, thinking of the long night ahead. No escape.

Stop fretting, she admonished herself as she turned into the upper hallway. Her room lay toward the end, close to the backstairs and the exit below. Clearly a plus in an emergency. A third exit next to the pantry downstairs led to Theresa's vegetable plot. Leo had no reason for anxiety about the blocked front entrance.

Anyway, being outside during a hurricane was more dangerous than inside.

Except for the creaking sounds from above and an eerie, strangely pitched whooshing and moaning, the corridor seemed deserted. The first three rooms on the same side as hers were slated for remodeling. Theresa planned to knock two of them into one with an ensuite bathroom just like Agnes's. Presumably, she'd accommodated the other guests in the rooms flanking the common bathroom.

At the thought of Carmen having to share the loo with four guys, Agnes's conscience pricked. The young woman must be livid. Was it unreasonable to refuse sharing the beautiful ensuite? No way, her ego protested. Not with Carmen so domineering and entitled. Besides, there was a powder room downstairs.

Like a genie conjured by Agnes' summons, Carmen emerged from the shared bathroom, still scolding someone inside. "Hurry up and quit whining. I want you in bed before that stuff kicks in."

Though Agnes couldn't hear a response, it must be Leo thus chided. Alerted by the flashlight, Carmen swung around and leaned against the doorjamb.

By the time Agnes drew near, the bathroom door was shut.

"Just getting something from my room," said Agnes in passing. "See you downstairs." Why explain? Agnes cursed her innate need to justify herself. She cringed thinking how Carmen must sneer behind her back.

When she reached her own door, the beam of her light caught on a dark shape on the floor. She bent for a closer look. Just a hat someone must have dropped. As she lifted it with pointed fingers, she saw it was a black balaclava. Probably from one of the guys.

Rather than taking it downstairs, she used the mouth slit to loop it onto the doorknob of the room across from hers. In the flashlight's beam, the metal knob surrounded by the black shroud gleamed uncannily like a faceless monk's head.

Dark, stormy nights surely breed strange fancies, she teased herself. Should write gothic horror stories. Still, she felt glad closing the door of her own sanctuary from the inside.

The atmosphere of the house or its guests was getting to her. Would it have been any better to face the storm alone with her hostess? Or the two of them in the company of Doug? Not a man to rely on in emergencies.

A vision of stalwart Kieran danced before her mind's eye. The much smaller Rob seemed quite as determined to be useful. Despite Carmen's obvious distrust of them, Agnes could see no reason why they'd be other than what they claimed. Stranded motorists on their way home. Harmless Islanders and hardworking arborists, to boot.

Her flashlight swept the Blue Room as Theresa labeled it. The weak light didn't do justice to the pleasing color palette. During daytime, the four-poster bed's blue patterned quilt echoed the pastel blue of the walls. Or had the quilt inspired Theresa's choices? Agnes wondered as she sat on the bed for a moment. Cream and white furniture and trims soothed and calmed the spirit.

Not so much tonight, though. A subtle movement of the drapes and the ever-present whining of the storm, punctuated by intermittent clattering on the window and walls, distracted her. An unseen evil was the worst. The hurricane held a fascination just as it frightened.

She padded across the rug and lifted the curtain from one side. The flashlight, left on the quilt, mirrored on the pane. First, she thought the darkness outside blocked her view. Then she realized the entire window was plastered with leaf fragments and plant debris that hammered the glass like tiny bullets. Still, she sensed a swaying movement beyond. Must be the trees bending to nature's force in incessant genuflection.

Bemused, Agnes dropped the curtain and went to the bathroom. No need yet to refill the toilet tank with water from the pails. Her bathroom had a gorgeously tiled glass-enclosed shower with a rain head she loved. How long would they be without power? Country life, where even running water depended on electricity for the well pump, sucked. When they filled canisters, pails, and the shared bathroom's tub in the afternoon, they hadn't counted on an army of guests who'd use the toilets. What a mess—literally—after everyone left.

Rinsing her hands with a bit of water from a plastic jug, Agnes encountered her face in the mirror. How odd it looked in the yellow glow from the averted flashlight? The creamy skin took on an unhealthy hue. Her rounded features, framed by heavy black-brown tresses, reminded her now of grotesque masks in ancient plays.

You're getting downright fanciful, she chided herself. Next thing you buy into shifter lore. The idea made her grin, which didn't improve the mirror image. Impatiently, she braided her hair and secured it with a couple of elastic twists.

Time's up, she told herself. Back into the fray.

Only when she reached the door did she remember intending to check the news. No matter. Dinner prep was waiting.

As she readied to step into the hallway, snatches of male voices caught her attention. One sounded enraged and unfamiliar. Curious, and with a caution that surprised her, she switched off the flash and poked her head around the doorjamb.

In the distance, by what she assumed to be the bathroom door, stood Leo, illuminated by the other man's LED torch. An empathic gesture caused the beam to flash upward. The light bounced off the man's glasses. With a frown, she realized it was Doug.

What in the world had Leo been doing all this time in a bathroom without running water? Or was it a return trip? He held on to the doorframe, a hand on each side as if he was barring Doug's entry. No wonder Doug was annoyed, his usually feeble voice distorted and deepened by anger.

"I need it now!" cried Leo. "I'll pay."

Whatever Doug replied was too low for Agnes to hear. As if he sensed being observed, his head swung around. His assertive stance collapsed into his customary, somewhat diffident, posture.

Nonetheless, he addressed Leo sternly. "I would not give you alcohol even if I had any. Alcohol and sedatives do not mix. That's final, young Leo. Do not bother me again."

Agnes completely agreed. Alcohol of any type would be a bad idea for this kid.

Leo's whine rose hysterically. "I don't want—"

Doug's hand shot up and cut him off. "That's quite enough of you, young Leo." Not waiting for any rejoinder, he stormed toward the lobby.

To avert Leo bugging her for booze, Agnes jerked back and shut her door softly. If she waited a few minutes, Leo might vanish.

Perched on the edge of the four-poster, she dug out her phone. No need for the flashlight. Batteries wouldn't last forever. It reminded her to check the phone's charge. Down to 72%. Should've recharged before the power outage. Turn it off now? What if her mother needed to reach her?

When she tried to check the news before texting her mom, she saw connectivity was waning. One bar and flickering. The browser didn't load. Her provider's cellular network was notoriously weak in this location. Now it was about to die.

Agnes's mouth went dry. Would they be cut off? Exasperated, she told herself, don't dramatize. Humans survived for millennia without a digital navel cord. She pocketed her mobile and made for the door.

Unlit flashlight in hand, she proceeded cautiously in case needy Leo lurked in the dark—and stopped in her tracks.

A tall figure loomed at a door closer to the lobby end of the corridor, the bulky hoodie vaguely illuminated by a phone screen's backlight. The phone's flash bounced off the metal doorknob.

Must be Kieran, having trouble with the bathroom door, she thought, as she groped behind her for her key to lock up. Best policy with odd strangers in the house.

Ready to hurry on, she faltered. Someone came from the lobby end, made visible by a sudden move of the tall guy's phone flash.

"What do you want in my room?" It was Doug. His tone strident.

"*Your* room? I wanted the bathroom."

Not Kieran, but Carmen.

Agnes kept motionless, intent on watching. At night, hulks look alike, she thought wryly.

"The bathroom is next door," said Doug. His tone suggested he didn't believe Carmen's was a genuine error.

Could someone obviously observant like this woman have missed the coy little brass image of a boy and girl on the bathroom door? The mobile's flash would bounce off the metal like it did with the doorknob. Was it intentional? Carmen's suspicious nature might well prompt her to snoop in the other guests' rooms. A creepy feeling stole over Agnes, imagining her own sanctuary thus invaded.

This raised her hackles. She walked down the hallway, head held high as if readying to tackle an unruly class.

Her approach did not go unnoticed. The beam of Carmen's flash aimed right at her face. Agnes shielded her eyes, saying gruffly, "Do you mind? Turn it down."

"Excuse me," said Doug and stepped close to his door, prompting Carmen to yield. He entered without a backward glance.

The bang of the door still in her ears, Agnes asked Carmen, "Is Leo in bed now? He still seemed upset a little while ago."

"Mind your own business," growled Carmen and left Agnes standing.

Chapter 6

When Agnes got back to the dimly lit kitchen, she found Theresa scuttling back and forth, muttering to herself.

"What's wrong?" asked Agnes. "I mean, besides the hurricane."

"It won't do," Theresa told the open fridge. "Four men! Mind you, Carmen has a healthy appetite, too." The glance she shot Agnes implied, 'And so do you.'

"I doubt Leo will eat much," consoled Agnes, wondering if holding the fridge open was a good idea. "Can't we stretch the pasta we cooked for salad? Plus, there's the quinoa."

"You can only add so many cans of tuna or salmon," sighed Theresa.

"Not to worry. It'll be alright. Beggars and so on, eh?" Agnes grinned. "Worst-case scenario, anyone still hungry gets a peanut butter sandwich."

"Mmm. Yummy," came Rob's voice from behind her. "Can I help? I'll splash on the jelly."

Rob's banter visibly restored their hostess's equanimity, Agnes acknowledged with a grateful smile.

The three of them worked well as a team. By the time Kieran joined them, they'd assembled a decent spread. No sign of Carmen, who'd promised to help. Agnes was glad the abrasive woman stayed with her partner. Needy Leo wanted her more than the kitchen crew. Did he really? Well, maybe Carmen was gentleness personified when alone with her mate.

Barely thought of, the woman sauntered down the stairs and sat down wordlessly instead of pitching in. Kieran, who returned from the pantry on a quest for wine, frowned at Carmen looking smug, sprawled back in a chair at the head of the harvest table.

"How's your fella doing? Not a bright idea leaving him up there alone," he said and placed the bottles at the other end, out of reach.

Carmen glared at him. "None of your business." She snorted. "Am I his nanny or what?"

Tut-tutting, Theresa ambled over. "Bet your Leo's in dreamland, dear. Them Seconal work like a charm. You gave him two tablets in one go, didn't you?"

Upon Carmen's "Yeah, sure," Theresa chuckled, adding, "That'll keep him dead to the world and the nasty wind for tonight."

The cousins exchanged a glance Agnes couldn't interpret. When Kieran cocked a brow and shrugged, a twinge of unease disturbed Agnes. Did they, too, worry about sedating someone who might be a habitual drug user? Or was there something else going on?

A sudden sense of being watched broke into her train of thought. It took a moment to discern Doug in the shadowy entrance to the downstairs hallway.

The man's sneaky habit of materializing silently unnerved her. Several times, she'd caught him observing the others keenly, only to shutter his gaze and morph into an ineffectual geezer when their glances connected.

There clearly was more to Douglas Junior than met the eye, she deduced.

"Why, it's Dougie," exclaimed Theresa as if the man's presence was a great surprise. "Have a seat. I was just about to send someone for you."

"Too kind," murmured Doug and tootled to a chair that backed on the kitchen.

"Dear me," cried Theresa, and rushed to the second armchair at the opposite table end from Carmen. "You must sit here at the head of the table. Oldest male gets the place of honor, my mum used to say."

Agnes's eyes shot up at this antediluvian sentiment.

Doug took it in his stride, though his pink hands fluttered as if to say he deserved no such thing. Agnes wasn't fooled when she saw his little smirk at Carmen. Of course, the head or foot of a rectangular table were arbitrary. His chair backed onto the entrance foyer while Carmen sat with her back to the main staircase and had the advantage of spotting anyone entering from outside. Slim chance of more visitors on this stormy night.

Soon, they gathered around the table, lit by the paraffin oil lamp and several trays with tea lights. A mild odor emanated from the vintage lamp and the candles.

Strange, thought Agnes. If it weren't for the inconvenience of the power outage, this would be quite romantic. The fare suited a picnic rather than a candlelit dinner, she admitted as they passed each other salads, cold meats, and condiments, accompanied by their hostess's apologetic monologue.

Agnes and the guys expressed their appreciation of Theresa's efforts and hospitality. Doug's head bobbed in agreement. Meanwhile, Carmen chewed on, minding her food more than her manners.

Several times, their commonplace conversation stuttered to a halt when thuds, snapping, and rumbling sounds from outside rose over the storm's shrieking, muffled insufficiently by drapes and wall insulation.

"Wind's changed direction. No good," said Kieran without expanding on the ominous comment.

As if to distract from the tempest assaulting their refuge, Theresa said, "Bet police won't catch the robbers in a hurry."

The remark apropos of nothing fell like a dead oak into their midst. All heads swiveled to regard the placid woman with varying degrees of astonishment.

Used to Theresa's leaps of conversational fancy and recalling the earlier mentioning of a hold-up, Agnes remarked, "Those robbers are just as hampered in their get-away as the police in their pursuit."

"True," Theresa allowed.

"What robbery might that be?" inquired Doug, placed somewhat in isolation at the far end.

The cousins sat at the center of the table, backs to the living room, across from Agnes and Theresa, who'd opted for chairs closest to the kitchen without having to face it. As the harvest table could easily seat a dozen, several seats remained empty toward either end.

Carmen, on her throne miles across from Doug, shot a haughty but fleeting gaze at him and addressed Theresa. "Cops are useless bums."

"Got a lot of experience, eh?" mocked Kieran, not bothering to look at her. Instead, he reached for the macaroni and tuna salad and held the bowl aloft. "Last call for seconds."

When no one took up the offer, Theresa smiled, saying, "You go right ahead, Kieran. Hard-working fellow needs a square meal." Apparently struck by another thought, she cried, "Goodness! You fellows must have gone right by where it happened. Did you see police?"

Kieran swilled down some pasta with water. "Eh? Where what happened?"

"My, the robbery, of course. That poor man shot today."

The cousins looked at each other. Rob's eyes squinted in puzzlement. "Where was that, ma'am?" he asked.

"Why, in Blyte. Right on Route 2 when you come down from Tignish."

"Did you call their *uncle*?" Carmen broke in, making it sound as though the cousins' uncle was fake.

Their hostess clasped a hand to her sagging chins. "Gee, I forgot all about it. Where's my head today?"

"Reckon Uncle's asleep by now," Kieran said.

Rob nodded. "Gets up with the birds and out like a light by seven-thirty."

A derisive hoot from Carmen met their remarks. "Yeah, right. How convenient."

"Never mind," said Theresa. "I can call in the morning."

"Fat lot of good that'll do," grumbled Carmen.

At the other end, Doug pinged his wineglass with a fork in a call to order. "Ahem." He cleared his throat twice. "Mrs. Mae, you were telling us about a robbery and shooting?"

Theresa bent forward to beam at the man. "Oh, yes, Dougie. Hadn't you heard the news?"

Doug's face remained bland. "I did not but would like to hear more." He folded his hands on the tabletop and assumed an air of polite interest.

"Yep, tell it all, ma'am," Rob chimed in. "Kieran and me are all ears."

A grin flitted over his cousin's rugged features, making his face rather attractive, Agnes noted in passing. Though she'd heard Theresa's cryptic remarks earlier, she too wanted to find out more.

The older woman's heightened color showed how much she enjoyed their eager attention. As Agnes expected, Carmen mimed boredom and loafed back in the wooden armchair, which creaked under the pressure of her brawny torso.

Oblivious of the young woman's blasé expression, Theresa launched into her tale. "Mind you," she began, "the news people never tell you much. The convenience store right in Blyte. You must drive by it on your way to your uncle."

Again, the guys exchanged puzzled frowns. "Not sure I ever noticed it," said Rob, while Kieran merely shrugged.

Cruisers would stick out like a beacon at sea, thought Agnes. During her weeks on the island, she'd wondered about the lack of any police presence on highways and in town. In Ontario, one frequently encountered cop cars.

Kieran's rough hand cradled a water glass. "Don't think we went through—what did you say?"

"Blyte with y and no gh," said Theresa. "Smack on Route 2."

"Yeah, no, doesn't ring a bell." Kieran shook his head. "Was a roundabout trip, anyway. Some detours at Elmsdale."

"Too bad," said Theresa, leaving Agnes unsure whether it referred to the detour or to missing all the excitement. Tongue clicking, Theresa went on, "What a thing to happen? The robbers shot the cashier, and off they went." Her hand shot up like the criminals had airlifted.

"Gosh, we missed that." Rob sounded more disappointed than shocked.

"Poor bugger," said Kieran. "Not what you'd expect around here. Hope they catch the bastards real quick."

"Did they make off with the takings?" Doug asked.

"That I couldn't say," admitted Theresa.

Agnes glanced around before asking, "Would they be after cash? People pay with credit or debit, don't they?"

"Plenty of folks pay cash around here," said Kieran. "Not like the city up Tignish way. Or anyplace away from town."

By city, Agnes assumed, he must mean Charlottetown, the island's and so the province's capital. With less than forty thousand inhabitants, it did its name credit as a town rather than a city by most standards.

"It looks so picturesque, but I read the island is far from immune to violent crime," said Agnes. A fan of stats, she'd read somewhere that PEI outstripped the national per capita average in this lamentable category. The most common crimes, however, were harassment and fraud rather than robbery. Its homicide rate was by far the lowest in Canada.

"Some heist," sneered Carmen. "A bloody grab-and-run at a Pop's Mart."

"Oh, you listened to the news?" asked Theresa. "Did they say more now?"

"I'm surprised they've named the store," said Agnes.

"How would I know?" Carmen rolled her eyes. "Damn places are all called Mom's and Pop's. What a hoot when they're run by Asians most times."

Cringing at the implied racial slur, Agnes turned to Theresa to ask, "I know you said the cashier was shot. But is he—"

The homely face wobbled in a headshake. "Poor man's dead. I feel that sorry for his family. Left behind a wife and kiddies, I bet. So sad."

The guys and Agnes agreed while skeptical. Carmen muttered, "You can't know that."

Reluctantly, Agnes's mind admitted Theresa was running ahead of the scanty facts. They hadn't listened to the news in hours. Their hostess appeared to go only by headline bites. Of course, the police usually were cagey about details in an ongoing investigation.

When it came to information gathering, Facebook was the island's grapevine, she'd discovered. That's where islanders asked anything from finding a plumber to the latest happenings.

Curious now, Agnes fished in her fleece sweater's pocket for her mobile. Her thumb opened Safari, but the browser didn't connect.

"Anyone get reception?" she asked. "Not even one bar on mine now."

Across from her, Rob and Kieran reached for their phones and checked.

"Nope. Nothing doing," said Rob.

"Same here," muttered his cousin.

Theresa tut-tutted. "Bet the tower toppled," she announced, quite cheerful. "It's too high up on that hill, I've always said."

"Got to be," Kieran said. "Doesn't work if it's blocked by woods or sits in lowland."

"Power outages and crazy weather like this knock the towers offline," said Rob. "Doesn't mean the tower itself tumbled."

"So you remembered your phones but not your wallets." One-track-mind Carmen harked back, her loud voice dripping with sarcasm. "Isn't that strange?"

"Believe it or not," retorted Kieran. "Frankly, I don't give a damn if you do."

That woman really got under the guy's skin, mused Agnes. From the corner of her eye, she noticed Doug watching the pair as if it were a televised debate. The little man hadn't bothered to check his own mobile.

But now Douglas Junior spoke in a surprisingly firm tone.

"So, we are cut off."

Chapter 7

An uncanny screech drew all eyes from Doug to the staircase. The man furrowed his brows, and his mouth contracted in a moue, Agnes noticed before she swung around to see hapless Leo descend.

"Not again," Kieran muttered across from her.

With the briefest of glances over her shoulder, Carmen hollered, "Shut up! You're such a bloody ninny."

The shout increased Leo's noisy keening. Carmen kept her back turned on her partner's distress. Swilling the dregs in her wineglass, she reached for the bottle.

Before Agnes could decide how to react, Theresa ambled to her feet. Clucking and shushing, she hustled Leo to a seat closest to Carmen, cajoling him with, "Poor lamb. You need a nice supper. That'll perk you up."

"I don't wanna eat," whined Leo. "I'm freezing." His whole body shook and shivered.

"Tea, then," Theresa diagnosed. "Strong and sweet. Warm you right up. Got plenty of hot water in the jugs."

"I'll make it." Agnes jumped up, worried Theresa might add a shot of brandy if left to her own devices. "Everyone finished?" she added and grabbed empty dishes to take along to the sink. They'd lingered over their make-shift dinner long enough, she felt.

"Get me that tea, and I'll tuck him back in bed," said Carmen as if Leo were a recalcitrant toddler.

He sure acted like one, Agnes silently admitted when he launched into another bawl. "I don't wanna go up there. It's spooky. Cold like a grave."

"C'mon, man. Get a grip," Rob coaxed but seemed to suppress a grin. "That's pretty fanciful. Just the storm howling. Old houses get chilly with the wind."

Focused now on pouring hot water from a thermos into a mug, Agnes heard him add, as if not to insult Theresa, "Ours is the same at home."

"Wait 'til win'ner," Kieran muttered. "Gets real bad——"

Whatever he might have added got drowned in Leo's cry, "I wanna go home!"

"If wishes were fishes, we'd be swimming in riches," said Doug, watching from the end of the table.

"Oh, you—you—" Leo's voice stumbled as he lashed out. "All your fault!"

"What the heck has he got to do with it?" Rob laughed.

Still swiveling a tea bag in the mug to speed the brewing, Agnes shook her head at Leo's non sequitur attack on Douglas Junior. Twilight of the idol, she thought wryly as she watched, her back against the kitchen counter. Was Leo's enchantment with his hero waning?

She almost spilled the tea when Carmen shouted, "Quit it!" and slapped the tabletop, rattling dishes and glasses and the rest of the company.

"Oi!" Kieran's long arm reached and steadied the cylinder of the oil lamp.

Rob's palm flew up, "Whoa. Take it easy, will you?"

Their hostess, who still stood behind Leo's chair, placed protective hands on his shoulders. "Shhh, you'll be all comfy soon. I've got some warm blankets for you. We'll tuck you in with a nice hot tea and some cookies."

Struck by the grotesqueness of this remedy for Leo's ills, Agnes had to bite her lips not to join in Rob's ill-suppressed guffawing. His cousin remained serious. The frown Kieran leveled at Leo struck Agnes as assessing rather than exasperated.

Carmen had pushed her chair back as if to disassociate herself from the company or from any responsibility for her partner. Yet, her crossed arms and clenched jaw spoke of sizzling anger.

"Be back in a tick with the blankets," said Theresa. With a last pat on Leo's shoulders, she shuffled toward the door to her own quarters. A flashlight she must have carried in her pocket lit up and threw the furniture into relief.

Astonished, Agnes saw Leo leap to his feet and scurry after their hostess. Must be desperate for the warmth of a wooly blanket. Or for motherly company, she guessed. She noticed Kieran gaze after Leo and shake his head as if something was bothering him.

Rob rose and slapped his hunky cousin's back. "Right. Let's give Agnes a hand and get things sorted."

At least someone cares, Agnes thought with a glance at Carmen, still loafing back in the armchair. Doug, at the opposite end of the long table, had retired back into the shadows. No help to anyone these two.

Agnes sighed, tossed the tea bag into a compost bin, and carried the mug over to the seat vacated by Leo. Carmen toyed with a cell phone, ignoring everyone. Maybe the woman loaded her device with off-line entertainment apps. Reckless to waste battery life during the outage.

When Agnes collected Doug's empty plate, she caught him darting surreptitious glances at Carmen. He lowered his gaze to contemplate his hands, folded like in prayer on the tabletop.

"May I remove your dishes?" she asked politely.

"How kind," he murmured but made no move to help.

So be it, thought Agnes and joined Kieran, who scraped food debris from plates and bowls into the compost. Together with Rob, they cleaned dishes haphazardly, stacking them in the dishwasher and on the counter for a thorough wash when electricity was restored. Conversationally, Agnes asked about their hometown but received monosyllabic responses. Rob looked drained. From her impression, Kieran didn't indulge in small talk, anyway.

The screech of chair legs on the wood floor ripped Agnes out of her idle musings. Like her, the guys interrupted the tidying to watch.

Carmen rose, growling, "What the hell's going on? They've been ages."

Not waiting for anyone's response, the woman strode across the living room and barged into Theresa's private quarters without knocking.

Though Agnes had lost track of time, she figured Theresa and Leo had left at least ten minutes ago. She voiced her unease. "I hope he didn't pass out."

"Better go check," Rob told his cousin.

Kieran nodded and already hastened after Carmen before Agnes could act.

"I think Theresa might prefer me to—" She broke off when Rob shook his head with a friendly smile.

"Nah, no worries, Agnes. Kieran's your man for emergencies. He can handle the kid."

"Still… Seems better—"

"Kieran's a volunteer firefighter. They get basic first responder training." Rob's tone showed how proud he was of his cousin.

"Oh? That's a piece of luck," she admitted with genuine relief. No wonder Kieran was a man of action.

A load off Theresa's shoulders, Agnes reflected, to have someone trained for emergencies with them during this stormy night. Plus, it spoke well for these stranded motorists, who'd shared next to nothing about their lives. Except, of course, about helping the elusive uncle in Tignish prepare for the hurricane.

The storm's eerie swooshing and shrieking had become a background symphony, punctuated by intermittent crashes, just when Agnes hoped it was subsiding into a mere gale.

Voices from behind announced the return of the others. The assortment of blankets and duvets they brought certainly needed more than one person to carry. Looked like Theresa was preparing them for a polar expedition.

Little showed of Leo's skinny frame wrapped from head to toe in an off-white, multi-striped Hudson Bay blanket that his fingers clutched tightly under his chin.

Carmen held a bundle of woolen blankets tucked under her arm. Her other hand steered Leo to the table.

Surprised, Agnes saw Doug scurry from the chair Leo had previously sat on. He must have switched seats while she and Rob had finished the cleanup. Or maybe the man meant to go upstairs but changed his mind.

Now, he beat a retreat when Carmen glared at him. She pushed Leo into the vacated seat, ordering, "Drink your tea and up you go."

"I don't want tea," whined Leo and shoved at the mug. Carmen's large hand grabbed it in a practiced reflex.

"Drink," she hissed at him.

Still grumbling, Leo downed what Agnes feared must be too tepid to warm him up.

He'd hardly finished when Carmen heaved him to a stand, swaddled him tighter in his blanket like an infant, and shepherded him up the stairs.

"Thanks, dear, for cleaning up," Agnes heard Theresa say by her side.

Too engrossed in watching the young couple's dysfunctional interaction, she hadn't noticed the older woman's approach. With a start, she realized how upset and exhausted Theresa appeared.

"Oh, the guys did most of it," Agnes told her. "Are you okay? Did Leo act up? Or Carmen?"

"It's nothing." Theresa's tone and dismissive hand wave failed to convince Agnes. Deep worry lines puckered the woman's usually placid features when she aimlessly straightened canisters on the kitchen counter. "It'll blow over," she mumbled as if to herself.

No wonder their hostess appeared frazzled, thought Agnes. What a responsibility to house volatile strangers under your roof while a hurricane ransacked the island. With every splintering crash, Theresa must keenly feel the brunt of the worry and acutely fear for their and her home's safety. After all, Theresa's livelihood was tied to her B&B's prosperity and the well-being of her guests.

"I'm so sorry, Theresa. All this must be rather tough on you," Agnes said. "Having us here and Leo to contend with. I'm sure he'll be alright once he gets some sleep."

The older woman nodded. A firm smile pasted on her lips despite the worried eyes; she spoke upbeat. "Just what the doctor ordered for all of us. Isn't that right, Kieran?"

The cousins, who'd been conferring quietly by the living room window, came to join them.

"Sorry, didn't catch that, ma'am," said Kieran, his face half-hidden by a bulky armful of blankets and a duvet.

"Get some sleep. Best thing for us, I said just now." Theresa's hand covered her mouth as if to stifle a yawn. "It's been a long day."

Far from sure sleep could be courted tonight, Agnes nodded and mimed a little yawn just for their hostess's sake. Unless the rest of them settled upstairs, Theresa wouldn't retire to her bedsit.

"Too right," Agnes mumbled, palm to her mouth. "I'm bushed. Have a good night, everyone." Catching Rob's grin at the irony of such wishes with the windows rattling, she added, "Well, we can but try."

Kieran seemed absorbed by his own thoughts. To Theresa he said, "If you don't mind, ma'am, Rob and me do a quick tour. See all's safe."

"How kind! You're a real help. But you must call me Theresa. No more ma'aming me now that we got to know each other."

Pleased to see Theresa back to her easy-going self, Agnes felt relieved. During her weeks at the B&B, the older woman was such a solid presence, unflapped by minor crises like malfunctioning plumbing or rabbits stealing the last kale in the veggie plot. Only the fear of foxes attacking her precious hens could rattle Theresa.

"Righto," said Rob. "We were just thinking, Theresa. Do you have a chainsaw?"

Both Agnes and Theresa's brows went up.

"Now?" Theresa voiced Agnes's own reaction. "I'm not sure…"

"For tomorrow, we meant," Rob explained. "Your drive's bound to be blocked like out front."

"Reckon the tree down by the hollow's a goner, for sure,"

muttered Kieran somewhat obscurely. "Leaned low when we came up."

"Oh, my! Bet it's the old hemlock by the brook. Floods the drive time and again."

"Poor drainage," Kieran said.

"The roots will be undermined, then," said Rob. "Those big suckers have shallow roots and topple easily."

Kieran stuck to the topic. "About the chainsaw."

"There's one in the storage room by the backdoor," said Theresa. "Mind you, the fuel cans are out in the shed. Can't store gasoline on the premises."

"Sure can't," agreed the volunteer firefighter. "Against safety rules. We'll see to it first thing."

Another blast of wind assaulted the windows on the far side of the living room. Distracted, their glances veered in that direction.

Jutting his chin at the curtains that moved in the draft, Kieran added, "If all goes well."

Chapter 8

The last thing Agnes needed was a gloom and doom prognosis from the stalwart Kieran. Thus far, he'd seemed a down-to-earth realist. If he feared the night might not end well, their situation was dire, indeed.

Her hand already on the banister, she stopped on the bottom step when she heard him say, "Got a battery radio, ma'am? Mind we listen to updates on the hurricane?"

"Goodness! Where's my brain?" came Theresa's reply. "It's on the sideboard."

Not having used a radio anywhere but in her car, Agnes hadn't thought of it either. Curious now, she leaned against the newel post while Theresa hobbled to fetch it from the living room.

It took some noisy tuning for Kieran to zoom in on a local station. Still, the crackling static was pretty awful. A man's voice faded in and out.

What time was it, anyway? Agnes wondered, having lost any sense of it in the gloom of the cavernous space lit merely by the oil lamp and a few tea lights. Her near-useless mobile told her it was minutes to the hour. The nine o'clock news should come on soon.

From the snatches they caught, the weather dominated the broadcast.

'…speeds exceeding 140 km per hour, increasing … tidal surges … 10 to 12 meters … north shore.'

"Not good," said Kieran.

"Oh dear. Bet those poor folks up the gulf shore wish they'd moved inland," said their hostess and sank into a chair. Both elbows planted on the tabletop, she clutched her cheeks, mouth slightly open.

Then, she added with some satisfaction, "I'm that glad I bought this dear place far away from the water. Mind you, they've got the nicer view up there."

Agnes couldn't help grinning at Theresa's way of looking at the world. Though, far from the water was relative. As the crow flies, they were probably a mere 10 or 15 miles from the coast to the north and south. At the narrowest point, the island's width spanned less than four miles.

'Emergency shelters open …' interrupted the announcer's voice in a loud burst. 'In Queens County … Charlottetown…'

He rattled off an endless list that washed over Agnes's head. She'd no idea where most of those places were. It seemed many were community centers, presumably equipped with generators.

"Do they provide beds?" she asked, just out of curiosity.

"Yeah, no. It's for warm-up and a safe spot," said Kieran.

"People can charge their phones and stuff. Camping cots, too, if you're lucky," Rob put in. "Or BYO."

"Fat lot of good that'll do. Jeez, we can't even get out of this dump."

Agnes spun around to see Carmen loom behind her on the stairs. Shocked at the young woman's hurtful words and ungratefulness to their hostess, she said, "This B&B is lovely. Doesn't matter where you are tonight. The man said most of PEI is without power."

"Not if they've got generators," retorted Carmen. "Bloody pricey, and not even a hot bath." Over Agnes's head, she glared at Theresa. "Why doesn't she buy a generator? If she stays open all year."

"Quit your—" Kieran broke off when Rob nudged him.

Dismayed, Agnes watched Theresa's face pucker as if ready to cry. Their hostess's voice was none too steady when she said, "I'm not charging any of you tonight. Didn't I tell you? Generators don't grow on trees."

In the shadowy light cast by the oil lamp, Theresa wiped an arm across her eyes. The strain of the night seemed to age her. She craned her neck to appeal to Kieran, who stood on the other side of the table. "There's the old diesel generator in the shed. Came with the house, it did. Bet it hasn't been used in donkey years."

He shook his head. "Nothing doing tonight. Me and Rob can have a look see tomorrow. Doubt it's safe if it's old and rusted—"

At the sound of the news tune, he broke off and raised his hand. No one spoke.

When the news anchor came surprisingly clear now with snippets of world and national news, Carmen grumbled, "Who cares?" Yet, she remained loafing on the stairs behind Agnes.

Given the more pressing local situation, Agnes sort of agreed. Her mind tuned in and out, too preoccupied with immediate concerns. Vaguely, another presence registered. She glanced quickly over her shoulder and noticed Doug had joined them a few steps up on the staircase.

Figures, she thought. The man sure had a noiseless sneaking habit. Maybe at home it served him well when checking on his brood without disturbing their slumbers. Unless he snuck up on them to catch them in some forbidden act.

A sharp intake of breath from Carmen or Doug behind her interrupted Agnes's mental meanderings.

Just in time to hear the news anchor say, '...released further details. The police welcome any information about two individuals in the vicinity of the Pop Marts convenience store ... Main Street ... Sergeant ...'

"Fancy that," said Theresa. "You were right, Carmen. I must have missed the name earlier."

But the young woman shushed her. "Can't hear him. Turn it up."

Kieran shot her a glance and shrugged. A burst of static had Agnes cover her ears, and Theresa reel back in her chair.

"Jerk," Carmen commented.

"Could we listen to the news without interruptions?" said Doug, his voice loud and firm.

Agnes could imagine him at the head of the domestic dinner table saying just that and wondered what his wife was like. Was she used to the man's sudden shifts from self-effacing to sneaking alertness to authoritative command? Or did he reserve just one role for his home life?

Her wayward mind snapped to attention when she caught '... described as male ... dark jackets or sweaters ... clavas ...'

Agnes's head jerked up in reflex. She forced herself to relax.

Suddenly, the announcer's voice took on an uncanny clarity. '... approximately 6 feet to 6'2. The other person is estimated to be between 5'6 to 5'7. At least one suspect is armed. Police encourage the public to exercise caution and call the hotline—"

When a renewed burst of static drowned the words, Kieran abruptly downed the radio's volume to its lowest.

"That's it, I guess," said Rob and stretched his arms, hands linked high over his head. "Now we know."

Agnes, who hoped no one noticed her reaction to what must have been a mention of balaclavas, told herself not to be ridiculous. Of course, anyone robbing a place would be smart enough to cover their head and face.

Tons of ordinary folks wore these face mask hats. You see them all the time in winter. And with the wind chill...

But it's not winter yet, her reason interjected. True. Still, the cousins said they'd been trudging through the storm when their truck broke down.

"Thanks, ma'am." She saw Kieran push the radio across to Theresa. "Like I said, me and Rob have a quick gander before heading up. Make sure all's safe."

Rob rose slowly as if cramped from sitting and stood beside his cousin.

"About the right size," Agnes heard Carmen mutter close to her ear.

The same thought had hit her, too. Only she'd suppressed it impatiently.

"Nonsense," she whispered back. "They are totally ordinary guys."

"Whatever," said Carmen. "I'd lock my door if I was you. Sure as hell am locking mine."

Chapter 9

Minutes later, Agnes reached her own room. On an impulse, she'd given their hostess a shoulder hug before heading up. The older woman had looked so forlorn in the murky circle of light shed by the flickering lamp when Rob and Kieran left to do their round of the premises.

When Agnes climbed the stairs, Carmen and Doug were no longer there. Must have headed for their rooms while Agnes exchanged a few words with Theresa, who told her not to worry.

Carmen's "I'd lock my door" still rang in Agnes's ears as she slipped inside her sanctuary. Her flashlight's beam flickered on the metal door plate. Should she or not? What if the roof collapsed and, locked in, no one could rescue her?

Surely, Carmen was kidding. Or wanted to scare her for the heck of it. The chance of the fugitive robbers landing in this B&B was infinitesimally small.

They must shelter somewhere tonight, another part of her mind argued back. Yeah, but not here. Most likely, they made hell for leather for the Confederation Bridge and escaped to the mainland.

By now, these murderous louts were well into New Brunswick and hunkered down somewhere in that province. Might aim north for

Quebec. Or they fled west across the border into Maine. Unless, of course, there'd been some delay, and the bridge closed before they could get across.

Though her musings had taken Agnes mentally off-island, she remained physically rooted by the door.

This is ridiculous, she thought. As if a hurricane wasn't enough excitement, her mind latched onto Carmen's groundless suspicions like a junkie starved for a cheap crime fix.

Her sketchy island geography told her the road to the bridge in Borden was farther south along Route 1, not 2. So why would the robbers end up at Theresa's B&B on Route 2, which led to Charlottetown and continued to the island's easterly point?

Unless they were headed for the easterly coast. Like to Souris. Or Montague.

Like Kieran and Rob before their truck broke down.

"Nonsense," she said to the dark and empty room. And then, unspoken, they're just everyday guys. Not ruthless criminals. Cut it out and get some rest. If you can.

Yet, she turned the key. Resolutely, she readied for a watchful night.

Not even the Sirens' song would lull her into slumber. If only she could listen to some relaxation music instead of the ill-muffled rattling and tapping of the tempest against the fragile windowpanes.

A deafening crash and echoing vibrations of the bedstead shook her sleep-befuddled brain into awareness. Her torso shot bolt upright. Agnes's body sped well ahead of her mind, still fumbling its way into the pitch dark now.

Memory slowly kicked in as her hand already groped for the flashlight. Pray its batteries weren't dead.

Swinging her legs off the high four-poster, she tapped her stockinged feet on the rug in search of trainers. In wise aforethought, she'd changed into sweats rather than PJs for her rest and left shoes by the bed. A backpack with her laptop and some necessities stood at the ready by the door in case of an emergency exit.

The sound of splintering had ceased. The light beam found nothing amiss in her room. Nor did the ceiling look any different from when she stared up at it earlier. Only the draperies stirred. So they had before flicking off the light last night.

Another tree must have toppled, she assumed, and unearthed her useless cell phone. Too worried about leaving it behind in a hurried departure, she'd committed it to the depth of the sweatpants' pocket.

Still hours to go until daylight.

The night stretched endlessly before her mind's eye. Impossible to get back to sleep. Whatever crashed must have been too close for comfort to create such a racket. Not a good idea to ignore that even if the room looked unaffected.

She padded over to the window and peeked behind the drapery, mindful of the possibility of cracks in the panes.

Close to the window, the fury of the tempest screeched in her ears far louder than before.

In the flashlight's narrow beam, the glass proved as coated with dancing leaf fragments as before. No cracks as far as she could make out.

Theresa and she would have their work cut out washing the B&B's windows over the next few days once power, and so well water, were restored. No way Theresa could cope on her own with the aftermath of the hurricane.

The mundane reflection restored some sense of normality. She'd go downstairs for a herbal tea. If the much-lauded thermoses still held some hot water.

As she laced her trainers and grabbed a fleece jacket, Agnes thought of her mother. Hopefully, Sera was alright over in Halifax. One felt lost without digital communication. The cell phone showed no bars at all.

The room, so serene on other days with its blue and cream décor, suddenly appeared stifling in the gloom. Was it the thought of complete disconnect with the outside world that made her yearn for human company?

Besides, she mused, the living room sofa was close to Theresa's private quarters. Sera wanted her to support the older woman during the storm. Up here, she'd be useless to her kind hostess.

Buoyed by a sense of purpose, Agnes unlocked the door.

The hallway lay pitch-black. Was it her imagination, or had the keening of the storm increased? For a moment, she hesitated, glancing into the darkness toward the backstairs.

Should she check the window at that end? No point. Bound to be obstructed by debris like the one in her room.

As Agnes turned toward the main staircase instead, a faint light filtered from a door farther down. It hadn't been there a few seconds ago. Someone else was up and about.

Her flash caught on a figure stumbling out into the corridor.

Drat! Not Leo again, her mind griped. Should she turn tail and fade into her own room? You coward, she chided herself. Just say no if he asks for booze.

Braced by resolution, she went to meet him, then realized it was Rob staggering forward, face contorted in a frightful grimace.

Was he ill?

"Are you—"

His cry cut her off. "I can't get him out!" His arm pointed at the bathroom door from which a weak, greenish light emanated.

Before Agnes could say a word, Rob pivoted, one hand groping for the door frame.

She squeezed past him. The buffered light came from a torch, discarded on some clothes or towels on the floor.

At first, she thought the room was empty. A sour, pukey stench hit her nostrils. Her own light sweeping the narrow space, she stepped forward.

A cry escaped before her hand covered her mouth to suppress a gagging reflex. Still, she forced herself to approach the tub, tucked into a niche at the far end under the window.

She felt her fingers of her left hand dig into the soft flesh of her cheeks as she aimed the beam downward.

Face-down, floating in loathsome, fouled water, was a skinny figure. Whitish forearms thrown in stark relief by a dark top now clinging to the bony back, there was little doubt in her mind. Leo.

"Grab him by the shoulders," she ordered Rob, fighting for calm. "I'll take him around the middle."

It took a repeated effort to haul the slippery body over the rim of the high tub. Only concentrated willpower prevented her from chucking up into the tub like someone else already had done.

"Get Kieran," she told Rob, who seemed to regain his composure now that Leo lay stretched face-up on the cracked linoleum floor. The bloodshot eyes stared vacantly at the ceiling.

Her fingers searched the scrawny neck but found no pulse.

Drenched, just as Rob had been already when he staggered into the hallway, Agnes shivered from cold and dread. What a horrific thing to happen to poor Leo. Her mind reeled. Not another dead body on her watch! Did death stalk her?

The sound of heavy footsteps stopped her maudlin. Kieran strode in, Rob close on his heels.

Agnes scrambled to her feet to make room. She and Rob crowded by the sink while Kieran hunkered down and ministered to what Agnes feared was a dead body.

With Rob grabbing the abandoned torch from the floor and the weaker beam from Agnes's, they did their best to illuminate Leo's prone body for Kieran's CPR efforts. It wasn't a pleasant sight.

Her eyes fixed on the wall above the tub, Agnes's mind raced. "How did Leo end up in there?" she said out loud.

"I don't know. Just found him swimming in his puke."

No wonder Rob's voice sounded shaky, she thought. Even kind of forewarned, the sight of the floating body had jolted her.

"Was he already face-down?" she asked. Something didn't seem logical.

"Would you two shut up?" Kieran growled but remained bent over the unresponsive figure. "I can't hear if he's breathing."

"Sorry," she mumbled in reflex.

"Agnes. Get his mate," commanded Kieran. "Rob. Towels."

When she hesitated, saying, "I don't know——" he cut her off. "Go!"

No matter, there were only two or three options to figure out which room was Carmen's. Glancing back before leaving, she saw the guys huddled over the supine body.

She needn't have worried. Out in the hallway, her light beam merged with another. Carmen, dressed now in loose, light-colored sweats, was upon her before she'd gone a few steps. Too late to prepare Leo's partner gently for what lay ahead.

Still, she tried to slow Carmen by standing in her way. "Wait. I need to tell you something."

"What?"

The woman's snarl hardly registered in Agnes's ear, too concerned about the impact of her own message. "It's Leo. He's… He had an accident."

"Not again?" It sounded exasperated rather than anxious. "Did he pee his pants?"

"No—I mean, I don't know." Agnes stumbled over her words. "He's lying in there." She pointed to the bathroom. "I think he's—"

"What are you blabbing on about?" Carmen interrupted, sparing Agnes the need to utter the dreaded verdict. She felt sure Leo would never rise again.

Carmen pushed by, her elbow connecting with Agnes' shoulder.

On the bathroom's threshold, Carmen stopped dead, blocking Agnes's view.

"What the f—" Carmen swore. "What are you doing to him?"

"Shut up," hissed Kieran.

"Kieran's doing CPR," Agnes heard Rob say.

She tugged at the tall woman's sleeve. The material's mottled gray felt surprisingly soft.

"We found him in the tub," she said to the woman's back. "That is, Rob found him," she added for accuracy. "He must have felt sick and keeled over. Kieran's trying to revive him."

Stop babbling, she told herself. Something she'd said bothered her.

Carmen paid her no heed, anyway, and barged into the narrow confines of the tiny room. Two long strides had her looming over the guys.

"I'll fix him," she muttered incongruously. "Silly ass fainted again."

Such denial of reality Agnes found painful to witness.

"Get out of my way!"

Carmen's shout left Kieran unperturbed. "Your call," he said evenly and eased back on his haunches. Then, glanced up at the over-bearing woman.

His voice soft and colored with regret, he said, "I'm sorry. The kid's dead. Nothing I could do."

With a ferocious howl, Carmen sank to her knees. Her arm scooped up Leo's upper body as if he really were a weightless child. The other hand shoved against Rob's chest hard enough to send him from a crouch backward against the wall.

Agnes cringed when his back connected with a thud. At least, he'd ducked, chin to chest, and didn't bang his head.

In a well-honed reflex for a person of his size, Kieran had bounced to his feet and stepped back. The front of his long-sleeved top and jeans were covered with dark, wet patches. But nothing compared to Rob's clothes. He hunched on the tub's ledge, shivering in soaking wet garb.

Not good after the shock of finding Leo, Agnes thought. Their duffle bag probably held not much else to change into.

Her eyes veered back to Carmen, rocking the lifeless Leo like a mother comforting an ailing child. An agonizing sight.

Agnes's heart went out to the bereaved woman, who was now muttering something indiscernible.

Without warning, the broad face jerked up, its features distorted by pain or rage.

The cry reverberated in the tiny room.

"You've killed him!"

Chapter 10

"What's all this noise?" came a stern voice from behind Agnes. At the same time, the white glare of an LED torch flashed in circles over the scene.

Doug, of course. No other male left outside the bathroom.

From sheer habit, Agnes moved out of the way and squeezed into the tight space between the sink and doorjamb.

The dapper fellow, now dressed in a checkered housecoat, striped pajamas, and slippers, brushed past her to join them unasked.

Another anguished cry from Carmen greeted him. "They've killed him!" To which Douglas Junior clucked like one of Theresa's hens.

"That's wild," said Rob, hunkered on the tub's rim, hands pressed between his knees as if to still them.

With Kieran leaning against the wall by the toilet and Leo stretched out full-length, his upper body in Carmen's lap, the bathroom seemed far too tiny to hold them all. Yet, Agnes felt reluctant to obstruct the exit and remained jammed in her corner.

"Done all I could. Fella was past saving." For a moment, Kieran's head drooped.

Doug nodded slowly. To judge by his profile, he seemed to take in the scene. His head bowed, apparently in contemplation of the corpse on the floor around which puddles had formed and ran in rivulets towards the door. Gingerly, he sidestepped the one that threatened his shiny slippers.

He lifted his glance to Rob. Or eyed the bathtub. Agnes heard him murmur, "Drowned himself. Poor bugger."

It was to her rather than the guys he directed his question. "Would someone tell me what happened?"

Polite yet authoritative, his tone again struck her at odds with the self-effacing persona Doug usually sought to convey.

Still, she appreciated the matter-of-fact note that lessened the horror of it all.

"Rob found Leo submerged in the tub," she said. "It took the two of us to lift him out. Kieran tried CPR without success. We came too late to bring Leo back."

"Thank you. A most unfortunate accident." The fastidious expression matched the formal tone. It felt as if he'd accepted an underling's report as satisfactory.

He shook his head, dislodging the strands plastered to his pate. Did he gel his hair into obedience? Impatiently, Agnes pushed aside her mind's misplaced levity.

"Looks like it," muttered Kieran and glanced down at his cousin, who sat shivering in soaking wet clothes.

Maybe feeling under scrutiny, Rob raised his eyes. Agnes, too, had a hard time not staring at the poignant image of Carmen, rocking the limp and lifeless body.

There was something incongruously possessive about this tough, brawny woman cradling the drenched, bony shell of what had really been a young adult. Leo had acted like a petulant child only hours ago. In death, his eyes mercifully closed probably by Kieran, Leo's face seemed that of a man closer to his early twenties than his late teens.

She knew nothing about him or any of the other people, for that matter. The proverbial ships passing in the night. Or, in this case, wayfarers stuck for one night in an isolated B&B. Yet, even if they'd traded life stories, they'd still have no clue if any of it were true.

"… move him." Her mind occupied, she merely caught the tail end of Rob's words.

"Yes. He would be more comfortable in his own bed," said Doug.

"No!" cried Carmen with surprising vehemence. "That's my bed."

Jeez, Agnes's mind commented. Yet, she admitted in fairness that the idea would disturb her. Something else bothered her far more, however.

"Wouldn't it be better not to? I mean, in case of sudden death, the police and a coroner ought to…" Agnes didn't finish, recognizing it was a moot point. They'd moved the body already and had no way of contacting police or anyone else until phone service was restored or they could get out if the storm died down when daylight broke.

The sharp look Doug shot her melted into a bland expression. "It's upsetting. So undignified," he said.

"The kid's dead," muttered Kieran and pushed himself from the wall's support. "Right. More decent." Over Doug's head, he sought Agnes's attention. "Any of the rooms across open?"

Doug was not to be sidestepped. "If I may suggest, there is a single room at the end of the hallway. I'm sure our gentle landlady won't mind if the deceased rests there until appropriate arrangements can be made."

If the circumstances weren't so grim, Agnes might have grinned at such a formal speech uttered in the confines of a crowded bathroom. Though he was irritating, it was good someone took the reins. Yet she wondered at the priggish fellow's intimate knowledge of Theresa's place. Likely, their hostess had given him a tour during his stay.

When Theresa showed her over the premises, Agnes merely peeked into the uninspired, narrow room at the backstairs. Plain like a monk's cell, she recalled. A double-door linen closet separated it from her own room.

No one immediately reacted to Doug's suggestions. Carmen's head bent low over the dead man in her arms. Would she resist removal?

A movement from Kieran got Agnes's attention.

"Mind going down and tell the missus?" he asked. "Jeepers, must sleep like a log to miss all this."

With a start, Agnes agreed. How odd of Theresa to ignore Carmen's outcries? Perhaps sound didn't carry over the storm's racket. Plus, Theresa's quarters were on the main floor quite a ways off.

"Right. I'll break it to Theresa," she said, perplexed none of them thought of it before. Were they all subconsciously avoiding their hostess's unpredictable reactions?

"Thank you, young lady," Doug said.

Wasn't your idea, she wanted to shoot back but choked the knee-jerk response. The man irked her. His address smacked of condescension rather than courtesy.

In the hallway, she hesitated whether to use the backstairs but opted for the main staircase.

Only the storm's howling awaited her at the main level. The living room lay in darkness. Her flashlight didn't penetrate its shadowy depth. An army of killers could hide behind armchairs and drapes.

What a silly idea, she admonished herself. Don't get fanciful.

Leo had another fainting fit. A sad misfortune. Coincidence that it happened while chucking up into the tub. Or maybe violent vomiting spasms caused him to faint. The reek of puke had been strong in the tiny room up there.

Still…

Stop dawdling, she told herself. Focus on how to break the news gently.

Not looking right or left, she padded across the room. The cone of light aimed at the entrance to Theresa's private area.

Tapping the door with her knuckles brought no response. Kind of expected with the shrieking and swooshing from outside and the door next to a window.

Nothing for it but to barge in uninvited.

The doorknob yielded. Agnes breathed out noisily, relieved Theresa hadn't locked the communication door. There'd be no way to reach her. Tapping on windows from outside wasn't an option.

Once inside the musty-smelling hallway, she wished she'd asked Doug for his powerful LED torch. Nah, they needed all the light they could get upstairs.

An image of the guys' gruesome task flashed up and made her shiver.

She gave herself a mental shake. Right. Get on with things.

The weak beam was more than enough to locate the door of Theresa's bedsit. A light tap to forewarn the older woman, calling softly, "Theresa?" Then louder, "It's me. Agnes."

Her hand was raised for another rap when the door opened inward.

"You're still up, dear?" Her hostess didn't sound sleepy or startled.

"Er… yes. There's something I need to tell you." Agnes's mind registered, like herself and Carmen, Theresa wore comfortable sweats rather than a nightgown or PJs. A legend across her ample bosom read, 'B&B good.'

"Oh dear," said Theresa, stroking her gray curls. "Not the roof leaking, is it?"

"Er, no. The roof's fine. I guess. It's the kid. I mean, Leo."

"Not again! That scaredy cat—"

"I'm afraid he's had an accident. Er, he's dead." Her dismay at putting it so bluntly was misplaced. Was it just her imagination? The older woman's shoulders seemed to relax, and a flash of relief crossed her homely features.

"Good gracious. That's terrible. The poor lamb." The voice certainly expressed concern. So did the clucking and head-wagging. "Dear me, whatever happened?"

"He fell into the bathtub upstairs. Rob found him drowned." Though Theresa would see the evidence in the tub soon enough, Agnes shrank from mentioning the fouled water they found the body in.

"Fainted again, I bet. Poor dear. An unlucky lad if I ever saw one." Tsk-tsking, Theresa stretched out a hand as if Agnes were about to run off.

"Stay for a tick. I'll snuff the lamp and come with you." With that, Theresa pushed the door shut from inside.

Left standing in the dark corridor, Agnes wondered again at her hostess's capricious reactions. She'd mentally prepared to deal with a distraught recipient of the shocking news. Clearly, running a B&B toughened and made you take distressing events in your stride.

"Did you leave him in the tub?" Theresa's question startled Agnes. She hadn't heard the door open behind her.

What an idea, though. "No, of course not," she said, sharper than intended. After a steadying breath, she explained, "Rob and I got him out. The guys were going to bring him to that small room by the backstairs. Was that alright?"

"Best place for him. We can't have him take up the bathroom. Not with four others needing it," Theresa said, practical as ever, and switched on a bright LED torch.

Agnes felt the older woman's surprisingly strong hand on her elbow, steering her toward the far end of the hallway.

"Backstairs," Theresa announced. "Shortest way. Mind you, never like to take guests up that way. Well, you're almost family, dear."

In the white LED beam, the narrow hallway looked far less sinister. Terribly dingy, though. Fixing up this entire place would take an awful lot. Time, mental and physical resources, and money. Could a seasonal business, like this B&B on PEI, bring in the revenue to undertake extensive renovations?

Then it hit her. A death on premises was deadly for business. Unless one aimed for ghoulish clientele. She'd witnessed the collateral damage at her best friend's ski lodge when someone died over the Christmas hols. Here, the death was even closer to home.

Could someone—like Carmen or Leo's parents—accuse and sue Theresa for negligence? A drowning death of a fully dressed young person in a bathtub would set investigative wheels turning. Was there a stipulation or a bylaw against leaving filled tubs unattended? Seemed far-fetched.

Still, a death is a death.

Their hostess supplied the prescription Seconal that doped Leo.

So why wasn't Theresa more worried about Leo's demise?

Chapter 11

When they reached the upper landing of the backstairs, Agnes paused on the top step while Theresa pulled the door open. Though awkward for entering the upper hallway, the door facilitated a quick emergency exit into the windowless stairwell.

She heard Theresa say, as if surprised, "Why, it's Dougie."

Sure enough, the man hovered in the doorway to the small bedroom closest to the backstairs. Raised voices emanated from that room. So, they'd shifted the body.

At Theresa's words, Doug swiveled around, seeming annoyed. The frown melted away, and he metamorphosed into his silly self, as her mind had dubbed what she felt certain was an act the man put on at will.

His, "Terrible. So shocking, dear lady," sounded an empty phrase to her ears. It was almost funny to hear him and Theresa tongue-click away in concert.

One glance past Doug into the cloister-like cell sobered Agnes. It also acted like a reality check on Theresa, whose equanimity crumbled at the sight of the body, only half covered by a blanket.

Agnes put a steadying palm under the older woman's arm. Still, Theresa clutched the doorframe as if afraid of fainting.

Apparently, they'd come at the tail end of a heated argument that the tiny room could hardly contain.

Kieran stood, arms crossed, his back against the single bed on which lay Leo as if arranged for sleep.

Facing the bed, her back against the long wall, loomed Carmen, dwarfing the narrow room. Dark patches discolored her cheeks. Legs wide and hands on her hips, her confrontational stance brooked no refusal when she cried, "I want his clothes off, I said. You can't stop me."

Not a muscle moved in Kieran's face. Being yelled at didn't faze him.

With exaggerated patience, he said, "And I told you ten times, no. You can't change his clothes. We've already interfered enough."

"He's right, you know," came Rob's voice.

With Carmen blocking her view, Agnes hadn't noticed him, wedged between a dresser and the window at the narrow head end of the room. He must have changed in a hurry after she went downstairs. His jeans and top looked dry.

Carmen whirled around and glared down at Rob. "You shut up. How do I know you didn't push him under?"

"He was already in the tub when I found him," said Rob. "Face down. Dead."

Theresa, who'd shaken off Agnes' supporting arm, now stood wringing her hands. An action mirrored by Doug in the most disconcerting way, Agnes saw when she looked over her shoulder.

Both he and she hadn't crossed the threshold when their hostess stepped forward.

"Oh dear, oh dear," Theresa lamented. "That poor lamb. All wet." She craned her neck to appeal to Kieran, whose height was magnified by the tiny room. "You don't mean to leave him there dripping wet? My, that's not decent."

"Exactly what I say," agreed Carmen. "Who are you to tell me what I can't do?" she hissed at Kieran's face. Mere inches apart, they were at eye level. If anything, Carmen had an inch on him.

This wasn't going anywhere. Or at least, nowhere good. Agnes noisily sucked air through clenched teeth. She cleared her throat to draw their attention.

Carmen's glare shifted to her while Kieran's shoulders sank in decompression.

He nodded when Agnes said, "Wouldn't it be best to cover Leo with the blanket and await the police tomorrow?" To Carmen, she added gently, "Leo won't notice. Wherever his spirit is, he's beyond the reach of physical comfort." Why did one grab at such straws when confronted with death?

The young woman was as unimpressed by such dubious consolation as Agnes's own mind.

Carmen's aggressive stance swayed fully toward Agnes. "Don't BS me," she growled. "I don't give a damn what the cops are gonna say. Or wait for it either."

Nor did their hostess wait. She simply grabbed the bunched-up blanket and, moving forward, pulled its hem toward Leo's face.

Either from deference to an older person or to Theresa's status as proprietress, Kieran mumbled, "Sorry" and squeezed into the tight window end of the room. Which made the cousins flank the dresser on each side like sentries on duty.

"Not his face," cried Carmen when Theresa shrouded the dead man's head.

"More decent," Theresa mumbled. "Bet he'd want it that way, the poor lamb."

Into Carmen's renewed outcry screeched a discordant siren everyone was familiar with. Albeit muffled from a distance, it was unmistakable. They instinctively reached for their cell phones. In vain. Without cellular network connection, their mobiles couldn't transmit any emergency alerts.

The notification system functioned from nationwide warnings of imminent threats to public safety to provincial and local alerts from government agencies or the police. In Agnes's home province, Ontario, and the Greater Toronto Area, the jarring, nerve-wracking sound had woken her several times when the police triggered child abduction alerts. But here, Agnes figured, it must be about the hurricane battering the island.

"Oh dear," cried Theresa, "Left the radio on, I bet. It'll run out of batteries."

"Good thing you left it on, ma'am," said Rob. "Radio's the only way they can reach folks now."

"Reckon it's hell out there," Kieran said. "Best go down. Basement's safest." He shooed them toward the door like a sheepdog rounding up his flock.

"But I don't have a basement," Theresa cried. "I'm real sorry. There's only crawlspace below." She eyed Kieran appraisingly. "You'll be on your hands and knees with your height. Carmen, too. The entrance is from the yard."

No way! Shouted Agnes's mind. With all her might, she suppressed a creeping claustrophobia at the thought of being trapped under a house. What if it collapsed? If things out there were so dire to trigger the emergency alert system, they were in far more danger from the hurricane than she'd assumed. Still, she'd rather face it above ground than buried under like a mole.

Fighting for calm, she said, "I'd rather take a chance and stay in the living room."

"Outdoor access is no good," said Kieran, and herded them along the corridor to the main staircase. "Not safe going out now."

"There's the pantry," mused Theresa, a finger tapping her flashy cheek as if to generate ideas. "Snug with so many of us. But it's got no windows. Safe as houses."

Yikes, not a great comparison under the circumstances, Agnes thought and grinned in an attack of gallows humor. Her voice shook when she offered, "I volunteer my space to the firstcomers. Close confinements aren't my thing."

Something else occurred to her and made her stop abruptly.

Rob, who'd followed close behind with Doug in the rear, almost bumped into her.

"You go ahead," she told the others. "I'll pop by my room. Need the loo."

When Doug gave her a sharp glance, she murmured, "Forgot my backpack."

A few steps ahead, Carmen pivoted. "I need a pee. You'll let me use your washroom. Eh?"

Didn't sound like a question. But, jeez, under the circumstances... Too cruel to expect her to ever use the bathroom again where Leo died.

"Of course. Goes without saying."

This garnered her another odd look from Doug. She moved aside to let him and Rob pass.

Without Doug's strong LED lighting the way from behind, the hallway sank back into dimness, hardly illuminated by Agnes's weak light. What did Carmen do with the torch she'd had earlier?

"Did you leave your—"

Kieran's voice from afar interrupted Agnes. "Don't be long. Not safe up here."

"Whatever," muttered Carmen.

Agnes waved, calling, "See you shortly."

Back at her own room, she unlocked and pushed the door wide for Carmen to pass.

Inside, away from the window, the tempest's discordant cacophony dulled to a menacing strain.

"Sorry, only got one flashlight," Agnes said. She cursed her need to apologize, yet aware she'd never kick the habit. "Should I get a candle?"

"Don't bother," said Carmen and dug a fat, rubberized torch from the bulky sweats, discolored by damp patches. They hung so loose Agnes hadn't noticed the bulging pocket before.

"You go ahead," Agnes said. "Bathroom's right there."

The bright beam of Carmen's light swept the room. Curiosity seemed to trump the call of nature, Agnes thought wryly.

"I so wanted this room." The young woman's face looked wistful as she gazed at the four-poster. Then, her features hardened, and she scowled at Agnes.

"If you'd let us have this room for tonight, Leo would be still alive."

The vicious tone, as much as the words, hit Agnes like a slap.

"What?" she cried. "That's insane." Suppressing her outrage, she said quietly, "I mean, I'm terribly sorry about your loss. Of course, I am. But I don't see—"

"Gotta be dense not to."

The beam pointed at Agnes cast Carmen's face into shadowy gloom. Yet Agnes felt her sneer. What a mercurial temperament. Or was it grief that sent this Amazon of a woman on an emotional roller coaster?

Still staring mesmerized at the tall figure who seemed larger than life behind the powerful torch, realization hit Agnes. Carmen was right.

Thoroughly shaken, Agnes whispered, "You mean… If you'd had this room with only a shower in the ensuite, Leo wouldn't have— Drowned, you think?"

"Exactly." Like a ruthless interrogator, Carmen pointed the beam right at Agnes.

Instinctively, Agnes's arm reached to shield her eyes.

"Don't do that," she said. A creeping sense of guilt weakened her voice and threatened to numb her. All she wanted was for this woman to be gone. Out of her room. Out of her life.

In a desperate attempt to ward off culpability, she said, "Accidents can happen anywhere." Though her mind warned her to spare the young woman pain, she groped for stronger arguments. "For all we know, he might have drowned himself. Or been crazed and sickened by the drugs he was on."

The light beam swayed and settled to form a circle on the rug. Distressed, Agnes watched Carmen's features twist into a strange grimace. She hadn't meant to hurt the grieving woman.

With a sudden hoot, Carmen broke into eerie laughter. At least, it sounded uncanny to Agnes.

"Carmen? Please," she tried to calm the woman as much as herself.

The laughter ceased abruptly in a snort. Not a trace of it in the hard voice that asked, "You're kidding, right? No way Leo killed himself."

Eyes narrowed and brows contracted, Carmen scrutinized Agnes's face. Like a judge's verdict, her words sounded final. "That pair Theresa took in killed Leo."

Though it was a mere repetition of Carmen's initial accusation of the cousins, it stunned Agnes in its matter-of-fact tone. An odd sense of relief flooded her.

If Rob killed Leo, then she wasn't implicated. Where there was a will to kill, an opportunity would arise one way or another. Irrelevant which room Leo and Carmen occupied.

Are you nuts? Her mind shrieked. You'd throw those cousins under the bus to save your piddling conscience?

"That's totally despicable."

"What is?" Carmen asked aggressively, making Agnes realize she'd blurted out her mind's venom.

"Accusing the cousins of murdering your partner," she said, unwilling to show a glimpse of her inner turmoil. "Not a shred of evidence for such a wild claim. Why in the world should Rob kill someone he's never met before? He's not a psychopath who kills at random." Though psychos probably believed to have a reason that counted as valid in their alternative universe.

"How do you know?" Carmen sneered down at her. "You've never met them before, either. You know F-all about them."

Without invitation, the hulky woman sank onto the bed, making the antique frame creak. At least, the appraising gaze came below eye level now and gave Agnes a reassuring, albeit slight, advantage in height.

The fact calmed her. Quite reasonably, she suggested, "It's fallacious to argue someone must be guilty *because* there's no contrary evidence."

"Spare me the lecture," Carmen jibed. "I can see plenty of reasons. The so-called cousins might kill anyone who gets in their way."

"That's wild," said Agnes, conscious of echoing Rob.

"Whatever." Carmen grabbed the torch she'd dumped on the quilt and pushed herself up. "Like I said, I want to use your washroom."

"Be my guest. I wasn't stopping you," snapped Agnes and immediately felt contrite. The bereaved deserved consideration even if their manners were corrosive.

Left alone after the bathroom door closed with a bang, Agnes became aware of the ever-present whirring and swishing that permeated the air like a terrible case of tinnitus. The pitch fluctuated, at times rising to a high siren whine.

Drained from the emotional scene, Agnes hunched on the armrest of an easy chair facing the window.

A night she'd be unlikely ever to forget, Agnes wagered. If they made it through.

She should hurry downstairs. Heed the emergency alert. Whatever its message might have been, it was bound to urge seeking shelter. But there was no shelter in this place.

What if there really was a killer amongst them? Carmen's unfounded accusations only crystalized her own misgivings. From the moment she'd seen Leo floating face-down in the filthy water, a growing sense of foreboding had pervaded her mind.

Carmen's voice cut into her ruminations. "All yours."

Wearily, Agnes rose as the outer door banged on Carmen's exit.

A strange sense of lethargy settled on Agnes. Yet underneath churned urgency. As she stripped off the sweats, yucky and damp from the rescue effort, her mind inevitably drifted to the image of the body in the tub.

The facts simply didn't jive. Say Leo was in the bathroom and suddenly felt sick. Why go past the toilet to chuck up in the tub filled with water? If at the sink, why not use that?

What if Leo felt disoriented from the sedative? Stumbles past the toilet and literally against the tub set across the end of the room under the window. What then?

He might faint while vomiting. He might fall forward instead of crumbling in a heap by the tub. If he'd fallen forward, he'd knock his head against the tiled window wall. Or against the outer ledge of the tub. He wouldn't nosedive sideways into the water, would he?

There'd been no bruise on his face. At least, she didn't notice any when they turned him over and laid him out on the linoleum. Nor did she see any before Theresa shrouded his face on his deathbed, so to speak.

Might he have sat on the tub's rim and keeled over? Perhaps. Would that pitch his legs over the edge and cause him to float face-down, making no attempt to flip over or climb out?

Agnes sighed as she fished for clean wool socks to go with the fresh sweats.

Though, sadly, this wasn't her first encounter with sudden death, she had no forensic expertise to draw on. All she could do was to reason through potential scenarios.

Still, the accident hypothesis appeared weak on closer scrutiny. Hence, either Leo drowned himself for whatever reason, or someone else did for him.

Of course, if crazed by drugs, he might have intended to take a bath fully clothed. A cold one? He'd already complained of being freezing cold. The bathroom was chilly and the water icy cold. Hard to believe it could appeal to Leo.

Why would anyone want to kill Leo? No matter how much he got on their nerves with his whining and weirdly childish behavior. You don't drown someone for that.

If killed he was, Rob would be the obvious culprit. He'd been the only one on the scene. Agnes shook her head. No. In their brief acquaintance, he'd shown zero psychopathic symptoms.

Met a lot of psychopaths, have you? Her mind scoffed. She brushed the thought away impatiently. Only to be struck by another.

What if Carmen's flights of fancy proved correct, and the cousins had robbed the convenience store in Blyte? And shot the cashier? Not that she believed for a moment either of the two was a ruthless killer. Plus, there was no connection to Leo.

Before her mind's eye arose the image of a silver knob poking through the mouth slit of a black balaclava. When she'd picked up the thing and draped it over the doorknob, she'd been sure it belonged to Kieran or Rob.

What if Leo had seen it and stumbled on other unequivocal evidence linking the cousins to the robbery?

How could that come about?

From her subconscious rose a shadowy figure. A light on another silvery doorknob. Carmen trying to get into Doug's room. If that had been an honest mistake, might a bumbling Leo not have stumbled into the cousins' room, taking it for his own? And found something?

Her sleuthing nose quivered. A sure sign she was on to something, she thought when she rubbed the itchy nostril.

It triggered deeper thought. Another scenario materialized. What if the suspicious Carmen intentionally searched their rooms, and it was she who found evidence? Say a gun? Or a stash of cash?

In that case, she might have told Leo. Drugged as he was, he blabbed inadvertently to Rob or Kieran. They eliminated him as a threat.

A chill crept over Agnes's body. Was that what Carmen meant by "plenty of reasons?"

If so, then Carmen was in mortal danger.

Chapter 12

Certain that time was running out, Agnes rummaged in the dresser for a slim jewelry box with a cherished gold necklace she'd be loath to lose if worse came to worst. A gift from her mother Sera. Agnes stuffed it into her backpack and made for the door.

Any minute, Theresa may come looking for her. Or send someone else up. She'd have precious little time to do what she'd determined on. No point locking the door now. With luck, the others had felt the same way.

The hallway appeared empty of human life. At this end, all doors were shut. Her weak flashlight beam created a murky gloom that didn't penetrate the shadowy depth farther down the corridor.

Sneak to the main staircase first, she figured. Make sure no one remained on this floor.

Treading lightly on wooly socks, she padded along. Someone had closed the bathroom door, she noticed. She'd have a closer look after.

Strange. Doug's door stood ajar. Only a hand-width, but still. Was he in there? Without light? Unlikely. Perhaps Doug was using the fatal bathroom. Yikes.

When she was steps from the lobby at the top of the main stairs, Agnes shielded her flash with her palm and avoided pointing it toward the stairwell. Last thing she wanted was to announce her presence.

From below floated snatches of Theresa's voice, muffled by the distance and the storm's rage, magnified by the windowed lobby's open space. A glance sufficed. The sitting area lay deserted.

Satisfied, Agnes slunk back. No sign of Doug.

Softly, she rapped on the door to make sure he wasn't resting in the dark.

No answer. The pressure of her hand had widened the gap. Her light flickered over furniture. Nothing moved inside.

Odd. He'd been so particular about keeping Carmen out of his room, and they'd heard him lock the door from inside. Like her, he must figure there was no point in locking up now.

Might as well have a quick peek. After all, Carmen thought it worthwhile—assuming the woman lied about mistaking Doug's door for the bathroom.

Cautiously, Agnes pushed the door wide and called, "Doug? Are you there?"

Still no response.

She inched forward and swept her light over the room. Unless Doug retreated into the disproportionally massive wardrobe, he wasn't home. Only half serious, she pointed the beam to the floor under the bed. She couldn't imagine prim and proper Douglas Junior joining the dust bunnies. At least, not voluntarily.

If he showed up from behind, she could always claim to have heard a groan or something in his room and bravely went to investigate.

The room appeared devoid of human presence in more senses than one. Neat as the proverbial pin. Never handy with needles, Agnes frowned at the simile her mind produced.

Did Doug pack up and take his luggage downstairs? Of course, he had carried nothing when they all left the room where Leo's body lay shrouded. Perhaps he came in here while she went into her own bedroom with Carmen.

Her beam traveled over the bed. White sheets tucked in severely held a dark wool blanket in a stranglehold, hotel-style. Or in military order. Theresa didn't arrange the bedding like that but preferred to plump up pillows on colorful quilts. A striped PJ sat accurately folded on the pillow.

So, Doug did come in to get dressed before heeding the emergency alert. Made perfect sense. He wasn't a man to meet his fate in PJ bottoms and a bathrobe.

A glass and a half-full plastic water bottle rested on the nightstand. Across from the bed was a small porcelain sink mounted on the wall. Useful when electricity powered the well pump. The glass shelf above the sink stood empty. Toothbrush and toiletries packed up or coyly hidden elsewhere. The latter would sync with Doug's prima facie personality.

Should she try the armoire? Her conscience balked at such an invasion of privacy. Yet, the odd fellow intrigued her. Plus, she reasoned, with a death on the premises and one she now deemed suspicious, even an innocuous-seeming fellow bore investigating.

She glanced toward the door she'd left open. It gaped back like a black hole. Any light, especially Doug's LED, would show from afar.

Conscious of overstepping boundaries that an innocent explanation might rectify, she sucked in a deep breath. Two steps took her to the double-doored wardrobe. The knobs on either side defied her efforts. Locked.

As she stared in perplexity, the keyhole plates blinked at her. She felt them sneer, pleased at foiling her attempt to violate the privacy they guarded. Put a lid on your fanciful imagination, she exhorted herself.

Doug's stuff must still be in there. He didn't prepare for a hasty exit, then. Perhaps he traveled with valuable sample merchandise or had more expensive clothes than she owned. Odder still to leave the room itself unlocked.

Bemused, she scurried over to the small desk beneath the window. The storm's noise wasn't as pronounced on this side of the house. Neither desk drawer yielded to her touch.

Annoyed at having taken an unnecessary risk of being caught snooping and wasting precious time on a fool's errand, Agnes slipped back into the dark corridor. A quick glance in both directions revealed no lights.

The cousins' room took precedence over examining the scene of crime, if the bathroom qualified for that appellation.

Steps away from her goal, a splintering crash shook the floor beneath her stockinged feet and startled her out of her wits.

Agnes gasped in fright. Ready to turn tail, she swept her light over the ceiling. Nothing amiss.

Unless she was mistaken, the tinkling mixed in with the reverberation sounded like vibrating glass. The window at the back stairs, she deduced. Her mind raced ahead of her feet and recalled the magnificent spruce that guarded the backdoor. Another goner? Another exit blocked?

Her palm flew up to cover her mouth, suppressing a cry.

Don't pull a Leo, she ordered herself, fighting down an urge to run. There's always the side door. Plus, plenty of windows to climb out of if necessary.

The idea of her unsporty body clambering over windowsills broke the panic spell.

Was it a need to prove bravery that propelled her forward? Or mere curiosity? Either way, she reasoned, checking the window over the backdoor would be a natural excuse if someone came running to get her. This might be her only chance to investigate the cousins' room.

At least Leo was beyond panicking after the horrendous crash rocking the tiny room that held his deathbed. Rob or Doug, who'd straggled out last, must have closed the door in deference to the dead.

She switched off her flash to avoid seeing only her own reflection. With a disconcerting sense of déjà vu, she lifted the curtain cautiously on one side, just in case the glass had cracked.

Though overall speckled thickly with plant matter, a broad strip of glass showed fairly clear diagonally across the panes. Spiky spruce branches must have swept over the glass like giant wipers when the tree toppled, taking the leaf pulp with them.

Odder still, she saw a white glare. Nose pressed against the pane, she made out a mass of branches, whipped by the storm. By the dissipating cone shape of the light below, she deduced someone pointed a beam outward from the window by the backdoor. A torch far stronger than hers.

Someone went to check for damage upon hearing the crash. The spruce must have scraped along the house wall without hitting the roof. Another lucky escape. For now.

Did they forget all about her? So much the better for her purpose.

Agnes hurried back along the corridor to the cousins' room. Part of her mind still insisted there was nothing sinister or criminal about them. Regular guys stuck here for the night by the vagaries of fate. Or, more precisely, by cutting their departure from their uncle's place in Tignish too fine for the cross-island trek back home. Even if they'd left earlier, their truck breaking down would have terminated their return trip.

Balaclavas were a dime a dozen. Or a buck at the dollar store. Probably, most of the Canadian rural population owned one. Black or dark blue seemed the preferred color whenever she'd encounter one in winter. Anyone with an outdoor job like the cousins would wear them in cold and inclement weather. Nothing suspicious about that.

By the time she reached the closed door, her rapid thought process had instilled some sense of proportion. The house still stood. As safe as houses, her hostess might add. The cousins were harmless and—truth be told—quite nice and attractive dudes.

A quick peek at their room was a mere precaution, she argued and drummed softly on the wooden frame. She didn't expect an answer. Anyone up here would have stormed into the hallway at the crash moments ago.

Her hand felt the silvery knob she'd draped the balaclava over earlier tonight. It was bare and felt chilly to the touch now. With hardly any pressure, it turned under her palm. The door swung inward.

A last glance along the hallway, her heart beating furiously, she slipped through the gap. And promptly knocked her backpack against the doorjamb.

"Shoot," she murmured and swore under her breath.

In for a dime… Still, better leave the door open for a quick retreat.

In the yellow beam, the room appeared deserted, like Doug's. But no military order here. Bed unmade, bedding in heaps, spilling onto the floor. Clothes strewn everywhere.

How the heck to detect anything in a hurry in this mess? Her mind grumbled. Where was the dratted duffle bag, the one lauded as waterproof that held all the cousins' gear?

A dark shape, half concealed by a green-patterned quilt at the foot of the queen-size bed, caught her eye.

On tiptoes, though she was sure to be alone, Agnes crept forward.

Then, a searing pain at the nape of her skull made her yelp.

One hand reaching up, Agnes twisted around.

Her vision blurred. Everything shuttered into blackness.

Chapter 13

Murmurs, ebbing and flowing like the tide rolling over a rocky beach, faded in and out. Agnes's mind groped at word fragments to cling to.

"…coming around." Someone familiar said.

Memory returned in disconnected split-second snatches. Kieran—horrific splintering—dead eyes staring…something eluded her…

The voice came closer. "Agnes? Can you hear me? No, don't move. It's me, Kieran."

She wanted to nod, but something warm and comforting restrained her movement.

"Easy. Try open your eyes if you can." His voice was calm.

The meaning seeped into her consciousness like an epiphany. This darkness was of her own making.

With an effort, she willed her lids to open. A sudden brightness blinded her.

"Jeepers! Don't point the flash at her," Kieran hissed.

Agnes felt his calloused yet warm hand slide from her forehead to cover her eyes.

"Mind if I check your pupils?" His voice soft again. He removed his hand.

She blinked slowly in agreement and felt gentle fingers widening her lids.

"Sorry, need to shine a light on them. Won't be that strong."

Moments later, the less intensive light moved away. Her pupils adjusted to the shadowy faces bobbing into her line of vision. Theresa's now, too.

Agnes tried to speak. Her lips formed words that wouldn't come.

Theresa didn't wait. "Goodness, dear. Did you ever scare us. Dead to the world, and me thinking, what will dear Sera say?"

The words acted like a tonic on Agnes. In the mellow light, memory returned. Power outage. Hurricane.

Hurricane lamp. Wasn't that what they called the oil lamps? Soft light. Didn't hurt your eyes.

Beside Theresa, another face crowded in. Short hair and muscled neck, like Kieran. Not a man. The full lips pouted. Carmen.

With recognition came garbled recollection. Spruce. Leo dead. Windows. Horrendous crash. Light outside.

Kieran's face, close again, blocked out the others. Something cooling and wet touched her dry lips, easing their pain.

"Just water," he said. "Clean washcloth. We'll get you a drink soon."

The soft cloth dabbed some more, was withdrawn, and reappeared, cooled again, placed across her forehead.

"Now relax for a bit," Kieran said. "Say if you need to chuck up or get worse. Wanna watch for concussion."

Her tongue felt parched against her palate. "What happened?" she managed to whisper.

"Dougie found you," came Theresa's cheerful voice. "Wasn't that lucky? Dead fainted in the hallway up there. Bet the scare with that poor boy was too much for you."

Some dim memory stirred.

Kieran's serious face retreated, replaced by Theresa's reddened countenance.

"Called us, Dougie did. Kieran carried you down here. Real strong he is." Theresa chuckled hen-like. "Must be all that firefighting."

The words triggered recollection. Agnes's head recalled the pain, her mind the darkness. Or was that her lids' doing? They'd closed of their own accord, blocking out the fleshy features so close they morphed into a grotesque mask.

Eyes pressed shut, Agnes focused on enunciating the words clearly. "I did not faint."

An overwhelming need to make them understand urged her on. "Or only after… they hit my head."

"Oh, my God. Dear! Don't say such things," cried Theresa.

"Could be you went down headfirst and hit the floor," said Kieran. "No damage I could see. Checked your head as a matter of course. Routine."

His face moved closer. "Any road, gotta watch for signs of concussion."

The more he heaped on, the more anxious Agnes grew. No one believed her. She needed to convince them.

"I felt it right here. Sharp pain." Her arm lifted to show where the blow caught her. The sudden movement brought on wooziness, making her give up after raising it mere inches.

"Whoa. Take it easy," Kieran said. "Best keep still for a while."

"What a drama queen." Carmen's loud, sharp voice hurt Agnes's head.

"Stuff it," hissed Kieran and rose.

Unable to move her head in fear of dizziness, Agnes could only see part of their bodies, now side by side. One in dark navy sweats, the other in jeans and a black top. An unmistakable vibe of antagonism issued from their stance, upping her anxiety.

"No one cares," cried Carmen. "She hogs all attention, and him lying up there. Dead and alone." The irate voice broke into a noisy sniff.

"Ah, but dearie. Your Leo won't notice. Snug as a bug," Theresa soothed.

"What do you know?" Carmen shrieked. "You—"

"Cut it out," Kieran interrupted.

Instead of unsettling her further, the nasty exchange brought clarity to Agnes's mind. A sudden insight. Dispassionate and remote, her brain drew its own conclusions.

Someone had tried to stun—or kill—her. That someone was right here in the house, even in this room. And she lay immobile and defenseless on the sofa.

When Kieran hunkered next to her, the brown eyes revealed nothing but concern. "Want me to have a look at you? You felt it in your neck?"

As his hand reached out, she shrank back against the soft cushion that yielded under the pressure of her cranium.

"No. No, it's okay," she stammered. "Must have dreamt it. I was out like a light."

His eyes narrowed. Did he sense her fear?

"Alright by me," he said. It didn't sound all right.

Alarmed now by her realization, her entire being focused on dissembling. They mustn't suspect she knew. Seem normal, her mind urged. Or what appears normal after a faint. Say something.

Necessity prompted the plea, "Need to drink. Please?"

"Brandy." Theresa peered over Kieran's shoulder. "That'll bring color to your cheeks, lovey. You look white like my best damask sheet."

"Booze's no good." Kieran vetoed the plan. "Water or tea won't hurt."

"Just as you say." Their hostess sounded huffed. "My dear mother, God rest her poor soul, used to say brandy settles the stomach and cures all ills."

She bent forward to pat Agnes' shoulder. "Don't you worry, pet. I'll make you a nice cup of strong tea with lots of sugar. My thermos keeps the water piping hot for 24 hours and then some. I bought the best."

With a satisfied nod, Theresa bustled out of sight.

Carmen must have left unnoticed.

Grateful for a moment of respite, Agnes drew a deep breath. She yearned for peace and quiet. Sleep would be wonderful. But she daren't close her lids. Any one of them might be a killer.

Beside her, Kieran asked quietly, "Does your head hurt badly?"

"I'm okay," she said, not wanting to draw renewed attention to the dull soreness at the base of her skull. "Just tired."

"Tell Rob if you feel sick." As Kieran rose, his large frame threw a gigantic shadow against the ceiling. "I'll get your tea."

"Kieran?" she called, addressing his back. "Thanks for looking after me."

His shoulders hunched in a slight shrug.

Unless it was he who knocked you out, reason suggested.

Against her best intentions, her lids drooped. Instead of welcome darkness, she sensed the room whirling. Frightened, she forced them open wide.

"How d'you feel?"

Her peripheral vision caught on another presence off to the side.

"Nah. Don't move. Easier for me to come closer. If you don't mind."

'Rob,' her mind supplied. She watched him inching a chair into her field of vision. In the soft light, his face seemed kindly. His disarming smile soothed.

"You sure look knocked out," he said lightly, like a figure of speech.

If only she could make him see she'd meant it literally. Too risky. Behind the friendly and helpful surface might lurk the devious mind of a killer.

She must play for time until she'd recovered her strength. Figure out who was a threat.

"A little woozy," she said, more to test her voice than to share. Did fear make her salivate? Her mouth no longer felt like crumpled paper.

"You would be, I guess. Fainting spells do that to you," Rob said, eyeing her closely. "Let us know if you feel nauseous."

Agnes concentrated on her innards for a moment before saying, "Not too bad."

As he nodded, she added, conversational-like, though she meant to get real answers, "Lucky I was found so fast." Not that she had an inkling of time passed.

"Eh?" Rob shifted in his seat.

"I remember everyone but me and Carmen went downstairs," she said, casting her glance to his hand that pulled at the finger joints of his opposing forefinger. She didn't even have to move her head to watch.

"Ah, I get you," he said but didn't elaborate.

If one of them came back up while she was in her bedroom, he could easily go to the cousins' room before she ever came out into the hallway. Anyone could. Who would, except for the cousins? He'd hide behind the door when she entered later. Land a well-aimed whack and stop her snooping.

Lids lowered to half-mast, she assessed Rob critically. Same size as her, but way stronger. Still, for a whacking job, Kieran was the likelier candidate. He'd have no trouble aiming a well-placed blow from his height.

Or had she bent down already, reaching for—? Something. Her memory was blank on that point.

Though it took her mind only seconds to puzzle over this, her scrutiny appeared to cause Rob discomfort. Or something else diverted his attention. His glance had shifted away to the far side of the living room.

"Storm's not letting up," he muttered. "Never saw a night like this."

"Wasn't the island struck by hurricanes before? Theresa mentioned it." Agnes recalled it dimly.

"Missed Dorian," Rob said, regret coloring his voice. "I was on a job in Quebec just then."

Enough digression, she figured. "What luck Doug was still upstairs and saw I'd passed out." The deep sigh she produced to mime relief even felt good. Her search of Doug's empty room was perfectly clear in her mind. There'd been no sign of the peculiar fellow.

Rob confirmed it, saying, "Actually, Theresa sent him to get you when that tree crashed. You'd been up there quite a while." His intense gaze rested on her face.

"Oh, I see. So, he got Kieran to render first aid, did he?" Surely, it must appear natural for her wanting to know, she reckoned.

"Kind of. Him and me checked the back door for damage after that humongous bang. Enough to frighten the living daylights out of a person." Again, he regarded her closely. "Scary stuff when you're alone up there. I'm not surprised you fainted."

She wasn't about to tell him what exactly she was doing when the evergreen toppled. "It shook the floor up there. Frightening," she agreed.

Let them go on assuming she'd fainted in the hallway. Of course, whoever hit her knew exactly where she'd been snooping. If she pretended partial amnesia, they might not whack her again.

As though it only occurred to her now, she said, "Ah, it was your light. I went to check the window. That's what kept me so long."

"Oh, you did? Pretty brave of you," said Rob, and added with a grin, "But you're rather brave, anyway. Aren't you?"

"Yeah, right. Superwoman. That's me." Agnes rolled her eyes and instantly regretted the movement. "Swooning like a Victorian damsel is sure no sign of bravery. Delayed shock, I guess."

Rob laughed softly. "Happens to the best of us. Anyway, Doug hollered down the backstairs for us to come up. He knew we'd gone check out the damage."

His fingers scratched his scalp on one side, messing up the dark hair even more. "By the way," he said soberly. "We all were lucky there. That giant of a spruce could have hit the roof."

"We sure were," she agreed. "The tree fell sideways, I guess. Its branches swiped right across the glass upstairs."

"Right on. Scraped along the house wall. We figure it flattened whatever's out back. Couldn't make sure. The trunk blocks the door."

"Good thing there's the side door by the pantry," said Agnes. "Plus, all the windows down here."

"For sure. No shortage of emergency exits. Was different for you, flat out in the hallway up there." Rob's glance shifted toward the kitchen. "Our knight in shining armor, aka Cousin Kieran, rode to the rescue."

"Don't spout bloody nonsense," growled Kieran.

With her limited perspective, Agnes hadn't noticed his return.

Rob's arms shot up to shield his head in mock fear of an attack.

"Brought your tea." The gruff tone struck Agnes as embarrassed rather than angry or unkind.

His other hand proffered something wrapped in a towel. "Here's a cold pack for your neck. No longer frozen, but it'll do."

While Rob held the tea mug, Kieran carefully maneuvered the cold pack to lay snug between the cushion and Agnes's neck.

"A little higher up," she murmured and thanked him for adjusting it.

"Want me to get Theresa to help you drink your tea?" he asked.

"Here already," their hostess chimed in. "Hand us some cushions, dearie."

Apparently, she meant Rob, who jumped up with a salute and a clipped "Yes, ma'am!"

"Sorry to give you all so much trouble," Agnes said as they elevated her back by slipping a couple of cushions beneath the one she rested on. Just enough for her to sip tea with Theresa's aid.

"Say if you feel dizzy," Kieran reminded her.

To her own surprise, the wooziness seemed to abate. Only prudent not to let on how she felt until her strength returned.

Feeding her sugary tea, Theresa smiled fondly at Agnes. "There now. That's better. Lovely color's coming back to your cheeks. And don't you worry about giving any trouble. Your dear mother never hesitated to help me out when I was down."

She chuckled and patted Agnes's hand. "Mind you," she added, "I'm not one to faint."

'Nor am I,' Agnes wanted to say but didn't.

Instead, she asked, "Where's Doug? I'd like to thank him for raising the alarm. What a lucky thing you sent him looking for me, Theresa."

The older woman beamed. She'd pulled Rob's vacated chair close to the sofa and sat nearly face-to-face with Agnes. Rob hovered next to Theresa while Kieran stood a little apart at the sofa's foot end.

"Gave me quite a turn. You up there, and that nasty wind toppling my lovely spruce." Her mouth puckered in disapproval of the elements' audacity. "I'll be missing it sorely come summer. Nothing like a spruce for shading a place, is what I say."

The chins wobbled vigorously when Theresa's head wagged in emphasis.

"Er… And Doug?" Agnes harked back.

"Dougie?" The counter-question expressed surprise. "Why, he's gone to fetch a warmer cardi. The house gone that cold. Wind's coming right at us now. Can you hear it, dear?"

'Gotta be deaf not to,' Agnes thought but muttered a polite "For sure."

Apart from the windows rattling and insistent tapping of God-knows-what on panes, the storm's snarling and roaring was hard to miss. Unless one was comatose. Or lay dead, like Leo upstairs.

Her involuntary attempt to glance at the windows had her wince.

"Ouch," said Rob. "Better keep your head still a little longer. Eh, Kieran?"

"Uh? What?" came the cousin's voice from the other end of the sofa. Not waiting for elucidation, Kieran asked, "Where's that woman gone off to again?"

The mellow light left his face in shadow. Agnes sensed anger in the gruff voice.

"Goodness. You're right," Theresa said. "Bet Carmen's gone up, too."

"Damn her if she tries to dress up her pal. Makes no sense," Kieran growled. "Dead dudes don't give a cuss."

Chapter 14

"None of your bloody business." Carmen's shout from the dark recesses of the living room startled not only Agnes.

Theresa clutched a hand to her chest, and Rob jerked upright.

Agnes couldn't see her but suspected the young woman entered through the door marked 'Private.'

Tsk-tsking at high speed, either at the offensive tone or at the invasion of her privacy, Theresa rose, red-faced.

The voice grew strident as Carmen approached. "So what if I put clean clothes on him? Leo hated yucky stuff."

Agnes could see her now, hands on hips, daring Kieran to dispute her right to do as she pleased.

"Just wait when the cops get here," Kieran said. "They'll tell you—"

"Fat chance," Carmen scoffed. "I'm not gonna wait for nothing."

"What the heck is that supposed to mean?" Carmen's abrasiveness had Kieran almost snarling.

Was it just Carmen's rude tone that got his goat? Agnes wondered.

She empathized with Carmen's feelings about Leo lying there in filthy, wet clothes, soiled by his puke. Who would want their loved ones in such a state, even in death?

Her reason sided with Kieran. They ought not interfere with the body beyond what their rescue attempt had warranted. The whole thing was deadly wrong.

One thing for sure, she thought. Kieran didn't sound as though he feared the cops. So much for casting him and Rob as fugitive robbers and would-be murderers.

Carmen, who'd ignored Kieran's question, strode past him to the kitchen. She hollered over her shoulder, "Any more food? I'm starving."

"Of course, dear," said Theresa and bustled after her.

Rob moved out of the way and stood by Kieran at the foot end of the sofa. Agnes heard them whispering but couldn't make out a word of it.

"Anyone else hungry?" Theresa called from the kitchen. "How about I rustle up a nice snack?"

As if in answer to the summons, Agnes' stomach gurgled, for once in queasiness.

Kieran came to crouch by her side. "Are you okay?" His voice was soft.

Anxious not show weakness, she claimed, "I feel much better already." If she joined them at the table, the guilty ones might betray themselves.

"You seem better," said Rob, regarding her, his head to one side.

"Well, one shouldn't take long to recover from a freak faint. Isn't that right, Dr. Kieran?" she said lightly. Except for the soreness at the base of her head, she might believe in a fainting episode.

"Uh? I'm no doctor. But, yeah, a healthy person should bounce back pretty fast from a faint, I reckon." He scrutinized her for a moment. "Want us to help you get up and move over to the table?"

Before she could consider, Rob scuttled in a funny gait around the sofa and sang out, "Lean on me…"

"Hey, take it easy," Kieran cautioned. "Sit up slowly, Agnes. One step at a time."

Agnes followed his instructions and planted her stocking feet on the floor. The guys offered an arm on each side.

She saw Carmen place a big bowl on the harvest table and watch them. "Bloody fuss about nothing," the woman jibed.

Part of Agnes's mind agreed. Only when she put her weight on both legs in a standing position did she sense soreness in her knees and shins. Must've fallen face-forward when the blow struck her. Of course, in a faint one might well pitch forward, she admitted silently.

Still... Two people fainting in the same place in quick succession for unconnected reasons? One into a filled bathtub and drown, the other while snooping where she'd no business to be? What were the odds?

The tiny head movement at her own musings caused no serious wooziness. A good sign.

"Here you go," said Rob and patted the cushions arranged in an armchair Kieran had dragged over from the table's head end.

"Thanks. You really shouldn't," Agnes said, a little distracted. The chair was Doug's. The man hadn't returned from his trip to fetch a warmer sweater.

When the cousins strolled over to lend Theresa a hand at the kitchen counter, Carmen came closer. She placed her arms straight on the table, palms flat, and leaned in. Her head lowered toward Agnes. "Tickles you pink that hunk at your beck and call, eh? Guess, at your age, a woman's lucky to get a guy's attention." The full lips twisted in a sneer.

Against her better judgment, the jibe riled Agnes.

Before her mind produced a snarky rejoinder, Carmen leaned yet closer to whisper, "If I was you, I'd watch my back. Other than Hunk there, no one here had a reason to floor you."

Speechless, Agnes stared at the broad face. Did Carmen, of all people, believe her?

"Er. I fainted." Her assertion lacked conviction.

With an incredulous eye roll, Carmen's glance shifted to the cousins, who approached loaded with foodstuff.

Theresa shuffled in the guys' wake with yet more food on a platter. "I'm real sorry. I can't offer you a proper meal."

"Doesn't look improper to me," Rob joked. "We don't often get a spread like this."

At other times, the sight would have foodie Agnes salivate. Platters piled high with cheese varieties, cold meats, veggie sticks, and fruit chunks, not to mention bread and crackers, were sumptuous fare by her standards. Right now, it held little appeal.

"Honest-to-God," said Theresa, "it was a blessing in disguise your truck broke down. What would I've done with all the food, I ask you? Spoils real quick when the power goes."

"What?" grunted Carmen. "You mean this stuff's gone bad?"

"Of course not, dear." Theresa sounded offended. "My fridge keeps cold for hours. Plus, I packed what spoils fast on ice. I'm just saying it won't keep cold forever." She looked at the cousins for support. "Not like winter where you leave it in a cooler box outside when the power goes."

"Power's off not even 8 hours," said Kieran. "On ice, it'll be fine."

"One can never be too careful with food." The sudden intrusion of Doug's voice at its primmest had them all gaping at the staircase.

As he stepped into the oil lamp's yellow glow, one arm at a jaunty angle behind his back, thumb and forefinger of the other hand tugging daintily at the corner of his mouth, he again vividly reminded Agnes of Hercule Poirot. Waxed moustache and a sleek cane were all Doug still needed.

He peregrinated the kitchen in mincing steps. What was this renewed role switch all about? Agnes wondered as he pulled out the other armchair and dragged it all the way back to the staircase end of the table. With a satisfied grunt, he sat down and surveyed the assembly.

When their hostess sank into her accustomed chair, closest to the kitchen, the cousins joined Agnes on either side.

For a moment, Carmen stood as if unsure. Her glance darted between Doug and the guys. At last, she strode to the foyer end of the table and picked a chair well away on Theresa's side.

"I thought she was starving," Kieran said aloud while offering Agnes the cheese platter.

"Goodness, dear. Do come join us," Theresa said, patting the chair next to her.

Agnes noticed the pleading gaze their hostess directed at the young woman.

"Lost my appetite," growled Carmen. "Yuck. It's the same grub you dished out for supper. I hate leftovers."

"Oh, no. All fresh." Theresa's upbeat tone wasn't convincing. "Cut just a few hours ago."

"Whatever." Carmen rocked back with her chair and, with deliberate disdain, unscrewed a water bottle she'd brought from the kitchen.

"Have some meat, Dougie. A man needs to keep up his strength." Theresa rose and grabbed the meat dish to serve him.

The fastidious little fellow threw up both palms in refusal. "Not for me, dear lady. Thank you kindly," he said, reverting to his usual thin voice. "I never take nourishment during the night."

"Dawn's not far off," remarked Kieran, eyes on his own lavishly loaded plate.

Doug didn't deign to comment but watched their hostess sink back into her chair with a dejected air. As though nothing had interrupted him, he remarked, "Prudence demands caution, however. Experience tells us meat and fish spoil easily. Isn't that so?"

His glance traveled from face to face and came to rest on Theresa's anxious features.

"Well... I'm sure—That is to say..." Their hostess's agitated voice stumbled along and ran out of steam.

An unusual loss for words in someone as talkative as Theresa, Agnes noted in surprise.

"Pass me the cold cuts, Kieran," Rob said louder than necessary. Spearing several slices of turkey and salami, he turned to face Doug. "There's always peanut butter, sir."

His dry but perfectly polite tone had Agnes chuckle. She covered it quickly with a cough into her sleeve.

Her amusement died when Doug said, "Food poisoning is no joking matter, young man. As I'm sure our admirable landlady knows only too well."

Theresa's cheeks and forehead went from puce to ashen.

What a thing to say as a dinner guest. Agnes thought, offended on

Theresa's behalf. No wonder the poor woman's hands fluttered up to clasp both cheeks in horror.

"Theresa is super careful," she said. "It's not her fault the power's off. Plus, it's up to each of us to eat or not to eat. Heck, Theresa's not charging you."

The older woman's grateful and eager nodding almost embarrassed Agnes more than her vehement outburst that could only increase the tension. Guilt mixed in. For she'd left the cheese on her plate untouched and barely nibbled at vegetable sticks and bread.

To reroute the table talk, and from genuine concern, she said to Carmen, "Let's hope the cell service gets restored in the morning. You must be anxious to contact Leo's family. What a terrible task for you."

"Me? No way. Not gonna happen." Carmen leaned back in her chair, clearly not interested in discussing it.

"Well, I guess you can pass on their contact info to the police and have them break the sad news," Agnes said.

"Nice kind of friend," muttered Kieran.

"Takes all kinds," said Rob, bending forward to shoot his cousin an appeasing glance.

"Hell, I'll be outta here first light," Carmen said. "Cops can find his folks."

"You mean you don't know where Leo's family lives?" Agnes asked. "Aren't you both Ontarians? I thought you mentioned that."

"Sure," Carmen drawled, visibly bored with the topic. "He's from somewhere up Bracebridge."

Cottage country, Agnes thought. Still, lots of folks hailed from Muskoka, the popular vacation area, a three-hour drive north of downtown Toronto.

While Carmen spoke, Theresa shifted restlessly in her seat but now seemed positively alarmed. "But, dear. You can't leave with your sweetheart's body lying in my bed. Cold as ice. Who will bury the poor lamb?"

Everyone stared from Theresa to Carmen, who merely shrugged and lifted her brows in a show of unconcern. What a change from the earlier scene of unconsolable grief, Agnes reflected. Perhaps she got it out of her system and is ready to move on, another voice in her brain suggested.

Was that why Carmen went back to Leo? Perform her own personal funerary rites, dressing his corpse in clean clothes? Saying goodbye in the privacy of that cloister-like cell up there?

Kieran's voice broke into Agnes's reverie.

"If you reckon on leaving with your motor anytime soon, you're sorely mistaken," he said, not looking at Carmen. "No chance in hell anyone getting out. Not until we clear the drive and then some."

"So what?" Carmen scoffed. "I'll hitch a ride on the highway."

"Good luck to you," Kieran muttered. Then to Rob, as if the matter were closed, "Pass me the cheese, will you?"

Afraid Theresa would be left to deal with the aftermath of what she herself deemed a suspicious death, Agnes wasn't ready to let go. "I hate to hark back to it, Carmen. But I think you'd better await the police. I'm sure we'll be able to find a way to contact them early this morning. They'd want to talk to you as Leo's partner. And about his next of kin."

"Duh? Didn't I tell you? Don't know his people. Never met them and wouldn't want to." A frown crossed the expansive forehead. With a thud, Carmen's chair landed on its front legs as she bent forward. "What do you mean? Partner?"

Agnes twitched impatiently. "Partner. Significant other. Whatever term you prefer."

"That sounds so stuck up. A boyfriend is all." Carmen grabbed a hold of the water bottle and took a swig, clearly no longer interested.

Across from Agnes, Theresa seemed relieved rather than more upset by Carmen's unwillingness to deal with Leo's death. Or was her stock of emotions simply exhausted? Agnes wondered. The night must seem endless to Theresa, bearing the brunt of the responsibility for her uninvited guests.

If Carmen really took off at first light, Theresa would have even more problems. There was also another practical matter, Agnes realized. "What about the SUV, Carmen? Is it Leo's, then?" As the woman intended to walk away from it, it might be.

"God, are you ever nosy. It's just a rental," she said, drumming her fingers on the tabletop. "I'll call them from the airport to come pick it up."

"I thought you planned on driving back to Ontario," Agnes said.

"What?" Carmen looked puzzled. The frown cleared in seconds. "Oh, that. I'm not gonna drive all the way on my own, will I? It's different now."

Which made sense, Agnes agreed. With two drivers taking turns, the 1000-mile-plus trip would be doable, though grueling, without an overnight break. Flights presumably resumed as soon as the hurricane had passed on.

Doug's throat-clearing redirected Agnes's attention. He sat straight as it befitted the head of a table, his hands folded on the tabletop.

His stern gaze fixed on Carmen. "If I may advise you, young lady, I strongly recommend awaiting the police's arrival. They will want to interview you."

"And who asked for your advice, boomer? Not me?" Her features were a mask of contempt. Then her eyes narrowed and shifted to Rob.

"If police want to question anyone, it's him. He found Leo in the tub." Her forefinger stabbed at Rob from afar. "Let them figure out if Leo was already dead. Or this jerk pushed him under."

Chapter 15

A sharp intake of breath had Agnes tear her eyes from Carmen and swivel to Rob. She saw him clench his fist around the knife he was holding. Good thing it was an ordinary flatware piece he'd been using to spread soft cheese. Cracker crumbs trickled pulverized from his other hand.

Enunciating each word in a flat tone, he said, "Your mate was dead." He stared down the length of the table at his accuser. "Don't you get it? We tried to save him. It was too late."

"That's what you say." Her powerful torso leaning in their direction, Carmen banged the water bottle on the tabletop. "I say no bloody chance Leo of drowned himself in a filthy tub. Or nowhere."

"But dear," cried Theresa. "We wouldn't say such terrible things about your sweetheart. Poor lamb wasn't feeling well. Didn't I tell you all along he looked peaky?"

"The young man fainted once before." Doug's thumb and forefinger straightening his eyewear at the hinge. "Irresponsible, letting him roam the dark hallway, ill as he was." His sweeping gaze accused them all.

"The dude wasn't sick." Head bent over his empty plate, Kieran sounded unfazed.

"Oh, but he was," insisted their hostess. "Far too thin." Reddened hands braced the edge of the table. With a grunt, she pushed her chair sideways to face Carmen. "Was your sweetheart anorexic, as they call it? Or that nasty disease where they—You know what I mean? Not nice to mention with the food on the table."

"What?" Carmen frowned at the older woman.

"Bulimia," Doug said, to Agnes' surprise.

"Don't kid yourself," Kieran cut in. "Guy was on drugs."

It echoed Agnes's own impression and had her nod in agreement, only to wish immediately she'd shown no overt sign. Besides, drug use didn't explain why Leo floated face-down in the tub. If this was really how Rob found him.

Vigorous tongue-clicking from across the table interrupted Agnes's cogitation.

Their hostess's cheeks burned, and the chins wobbled when she asserted, "My Seconal never harmed me. Heavens, two little pills give a body a good night's sleep."

Kieran pushed away his plate. "I wasn't talking sedatives, ma'am." In a patient tone, he explained, "Dude reeked of cannabis. Reckon he took hard drugs, too." From under his brow, he shot a glance at Carmen. "Told you he needed looking after."

"Me? Am I his bloody keeper?" Outrage mixed with scorn colored Carmen's deep voice. "You all talk like Leo was a little kid and me his mom."

This closely mirrored Agnes's earlier thoughts. Out of curiosity, but mostly to ease the tension, she said, "I think you're right, Carmen. Leo seemed deceptively young for his age. As do many of my students. Later, I figured, he must be at least 20." She didn't add it was in death his true age showed.

"21 come April," Carmen said, for once without rancor.

"Good gracious," Theresa chimed in. "And me thinking him a good five years younger than you, dear."

"Well, thanks a bunch. I'm not an old cow yet." Even from a relative distance, Agnes could see Carmen's plumb lips pout.

The older woman said sweetly, "Oh no, dear. You've got a long way to go before that."

Agnes hid a grin.

Though used to Theresa's conversation leaps and bounds, she did a double take when the woman favored Kieran with an excited twinkle, saying, "Now, I wonder. Would you be meaning that nasty stuff? Fantasy, they said on the news. A real crisis on the island."

She shook a finger at Agnes. "Remember the alert? We said so this afternoon."

Thoroughly confused frowns and eye rolls met this convoluted speech.

"You mean the emergency alert, ma'am?" Rob asked but garnered only a frown.

Light dawned for Agnes. "You mean Fentanyl, Theresa. The crisis the PEI health authorities warned about. Nothing to do with the hurricane emergency alert," she told the others. "Theresa mentioned it to Doug and me earlier. It was on Facebook and on the local news." Or was that before Doug's return?

Either way, Theresa beamed across at her. "That's right, Agnes dear."

"Would explain the kid's—sorry, Leo's—anxiety and mood changes," said Kieran, toying with his water glass. "Deadly stuff." Again, he scowled at Carmen. "Was that what he was on?"

"How would I know?" Carmen blustered. Yet Agnes saw her stiffen. "His quack prescribed some meds is all I know." She smirked. "Folks down here are so behind. Cannabis is legal in Canada. Has been for ages."

Well, not all that long, thought Agnes. Still, it was true enough. Plus, medicinal cannabis dated farther back. She sat back as the cousins leaned forward, exchanging grins.

"Gotta be kidding." Rob bent even farther to grin at Carmen. "Island folks backward about weed? Man, there were lineups when the first cannabis store opened in town." Then he sobered. "Not like legalizing the stuff made a mighty difference. Been around all along, eh, Kieran?"

Carmen pounced, even if only verbally. "So, that's your line. Now people pick it up with the groceries, and you guys had to switch."

"Hey, are you nuts?" cried Rob. "Us peddling dope? Not on your life!"

He might have saved his breath, thought Agnes, as Carmen dismissed the protest with a hoot. Agnes cast him a supportive glance. Did she feel protective toward Rob just because he was so much smaller than Carmen? After all, Agnes admitted to herself, she'd seriously cast him and Kieran as potential criminals. Though, every time she looked at them, the idea struck her as ridiculous.

"Your *cousin*," Carmen stressed the word in pointing at Kieran as if he were an impostor, "he's got access to drugs. Him a paramedic. Or so he claims."

"What?" Kieran wrinkled his nose like a rabbit sensing a noxious smell. "Where do you get that from? I'm with the volunteer firefighters in my hometown. I'm no paramedic."

"That's wild," commented Rob.

Weird, thought Agnes. Where did the paramedic notion come from? Then she recalled Rob mentioning Kieran's first aid training. Didn't make him a paramedic with access to a whole slew of meds. Carmen wasn't there when Rob told her while Kieran applied CPR to the lifeless Leo. Or did he tell her earlier? Confused, Agnes's mind admitted a bonk over the head affected memory and cogitation.

"Whatever." The rejoinder brushed aside any objections. "Fact is, we know f—all about you two. You blew in here out of nowhere. Anyone can turn up claiming their truck broke down, and no ID."

Crimson now, Theresa broke in. "But, Carmen, dear. You and Leo—"

Whatever the point, Carmen's vicious hiss, "It's all your fault," choked it off.

"I didn't…" their hostess's voice quavered.

"Leave Theresa alone." Fed up with Carmen's irrational lashing out, Agnes reverted to her commanding classroom persona. There was a limit to leeway for bereavement, she felt. Plus, doubts surfaced about how deeply Leo's death affected his erstwhile friend.

"She let them in," screeched Carmen, finger-pointing at their hostess.

"Good grief," cried Theresa. "What else could I do? Leave them out in the cold in that nasty wind?"

"The spy who came in from the cold." For once, Doug's words came loud and decisive.

"Eh?" Kieran craned his head past Agnes to frown at Doug.

"Never mind an old boomer." Doug's tone struck Agnes as sardonic, and his eyes twinkled. Or was that the light on his spectacles?

"A spy movie I enjoyed as a youngster," Doug said.

Was Doug alluding merely to the 'cold' prompt, or was he hinting at disseminating misinformation? The latter, Agnes dimly recalled from John le Carré's book, was the mission of the protagonist. If so, Doug might have a point. Anyone here might mislead intentionally.

If, however, it aimed to distract from Carmen's attack, it worked to some extent.

Rob grinned at his dapper neighbor. "Not just for boomers, sir. Kieran and me dig old movies. Cold war stuff's coming back." Instead of launching into politics, his glance went from face to face. "Fact is, anyone can be fake. Big cousin, here, and me grew up together. But we know nothing about any of you."

He pivoted in his chair to grin at Agnes. "Not even about you."

"Me?" Agnes grinned back. "That's simple. I'm from Toronto and teach this term at a college on the island. Look me up online. My CV chronicles my life for all to see."

"No internet," Kieran said.

"Hah, got you there." Rob laughed, clearly pleased with the big guy. "No internet, no proof. Just like us with the phone."

Glad to lighten the atmosphere—for now—Agnes countered, "CV's on my laptop. I'll show you. The battery's still full."

Doug shook a finger at her. "Ah, my dear young lady, curriculum vitae and resumés can be faked. Whatever is on your laptop does not count as evidence."

Taken aback, Agnes stared at the man. Was he serious or merely jesting? His bland expression gave nothing away.

Her eye fell on their hostess, who looked at a loss. Agnes grinned, saying, "Hey, I'm in luck. Theresa, you can vouch for me." And to Rob and Doug, "Theresa and my mother are friends."

"That's right, dearie." The older woman nodded, and her features softened in a wistful smile. "Your mom and me go back a long way."

"Exactly. Thanks, Theresa," Agnes said before Theresa could mention that she'd never met the daughter until a few weeks ago. One way or another, all seven of them were strangers.

"Satisfied?" she asked Rob, who gave her a thumbs up. To include the sullen Carmen, Agnes went on, "If you doubt a person's identity, an ID like a driver's license or passport won't work. Probably not that difficult acquiring faked ones. If someone is criminally minded, I mean. Ditto for one's online presence. You'd need to conduct extensive research and access to the relevant databases to prove an identity bogus."

"That is correct." Though Doug's voice was fastidious as ever, a smug expression crossed his features.

"What about you, sir?" Rob asked politely. "You came in from the cold, too, I bet." His engaging grin turned the question into a conversational gambit.

It made Agnes wonder. Had Rob also noticed the gent's odd personality splits? Eagerly, she waited for Doug to do more than merely clear his throat.

Their hostess's tut-tutting augured an imminent defense of Doug's honor.

Screeching chair legs diverted their attention to Carmen, who scooted back a foot or two from the table. Ostensibly pleased her little move put her into the limelight, even if it was the dim glow of a vintage oil lamp, the hunky woman took a swig from her water bottle.

Her stare pinned Douglas Junior like an insect. "Yeah," she drawled. "Who in hell are you anyways?"

An explosive sputter from Theresa made Agnes sit up. The woman looked ready to choke.

"You all right?" Agnes asked.

Their hostess paid no heed but twisted her torso toward Carmen as far as her chubby proportions allowed. "Mind your language." No endearment softened the speech. "I won't have you say spiteful things about my guests."

A bit late for such injunction, thought Agnes.

Admonishment delivered, and ignoring the knee-jerk "Whatever," Theresa turned the other way and beamed at Doug.

The man sat back, unperturbed. Hands interlaced on his cardigan-clad belly, he twiddled his thumbs.

Theresa waggled a finger at him. With an almost girly giggle, she announced, "I know all about you, Dougie."

A smile stretched Doug's tightly closed lips. Agnes noticed a frown ripple over the receding hairline. 'Dougie' was not amused.

Oblivious of the man's reaction, their hostess's motherly countenance regarded Rob and Kieran. "It's not the first time. Not by a long chalk. Dougie's stayed with me before. Such a respectable family man. Goodness," she cried, gazing at Doug again. "How your wife and kiddies must worry about you tonight."

"All five of them," Agnes filled in with a wry smile. Though, if they were still young children, most likely, they'd be fast asleep and ignorant of their sire's plight.

A complaisant expression smoothed Doug's features. "My dear Mrs. Mae, a little anxiety about the breadwinner never goes amiss. But the missus knows I'm in good hands."

The sentiments and his bow toward Theresa had Agnes suppress a groan.

Theresa preened. "Bet they got used to you being on the road a lot."

Next to Agnes, Rob fidgeted in his seat. Did the exchange make him wonder, too?

Yet, it was Kieran on her other side who commented. "Must be hard on your wife. Can't be a breeze coping with five nippers on her own."

Doug merely frowned at his pink hands as if their renewed thumb-twiddling came unexpectedly.

The shorter cousin pitched in, polite as ever. "What's your line of business, sir? If you don't mind me asking."

"Not at all, young man," Doug assured him magnanimously. "Call me an itinerant traveler. A small cog in a vast corporation. You know how it is."

"Eh? Actually, I don't," said Rob.

Like her, Agnes noticed, he appeared puzzled yet intrigued by the man's evasiveness.

"Traveling sounds fun," she said to Doug. "Which corporation do you work for?"

Again, the thin lips stretched into a smile that left the eyes unmoved. "That would be telling," he said coyly. "Against company policy, dear lady. We must tread carefully when investigating new territory." He put a forefinger to his lips. "Hush, hush, or the competition will pounce."

Agnes felt tempted to roll her eyes but suppressed the urge in deference to Theresa's favorite guest. Was the man having them on? Ludicrous to make a mystery of his job. Maybe he led such a mundane salesman's life he fantasized about being a spy like le Carré's heroes. Or was Doug a minor government underling of some sort? A boring bureaucrat? The 'investigate' might be a slip of the tongue.

"Where's home, then?" Kieran's voice interrupted her speculation.

"Winnipeg," cried Theresa as if she'd got the winning answer in a trivia challenge. "Isn't that right, Dougie?"

"Near enough, dear lady." Doug sketched another little bow in their hostess's direction.

"You're telling us f-all," boomed Carmen.

Focused on Doug and their end of the table, Agnes momentarily forgot the sixth member of their party. Not that their assembly of stranded wayfarers felt like partying, she thought ruefully.

Into Theresa's tsking, Doug said, "If you'll excuse me, Mrs. Mae, I shall retire to one of your cozy armchairs over there."

Theresa ambled to her feet. "Of course. Let me bring you a light. Pitch dark in the living room."

"Please, don't on my account. A little shut eye is just what I need. I'm not used to late hours like these youngsters here." He bounced up with surprising alacrity and moseyed into the shadows of the unlit room behind them.

"Bet we all feel tired," Theresa said. "I'll tidy here and put my feet up for a few minutes if no one needs me."

Rob jumped out of his seat. "Let us clean up, ma'am. Me and Kieran do it at home. You and Agnes get some rest."

Either Carmen didn't figure in this, or Rob knew better than to involve the volatile woman, Agnes assumed. The guys' stamina certainly exceeded her own.

Gratefully, she accepted the offer, saying, "Sweet of you. Thanks." And to their hostess, "May I use your bathroom, Theresa?"

"Come along, dear." As if another thought hit her, the older woman looked at Carmen and then told the cousins, "Mind that oil lamp. Catches fire real quick."

"Not to worry, ma'am," Rob assured her. "Never leave an open flame unattended. Eh, Kieran?"

His firefighter cousin didn't bother answering.

"Call me if you need me," Theresa reminded them, grabbed a flashlight, and lit the way through the shadowy living room.

Agnes hastened after her to the door marked 'Private.'

It wasn't the loo she needed urgently but a chat with their hostess away from prying ears.

Chapter 16

Once locked into Theresa's crummy bathroom and nature's call heeded, Agnes stood at the sink and contemplated her own image. The medicine cabinet's mirror was going blind with age.

One might blame the dark undereye circles and the patchy blotches marring her pale skin on the shaded flashlight's glimmer, she thought. Or on a sleepless night, too many frights, and a head bashing.

Her hand went up and gingerly explored the tender area at the base of her skull. She'd been darn lucky. Maybe the attacker intended to stun rather than kill. A warning?

Was it only her inattention, or had the storm's roar lessened? Hard to tell in this dingy cubbyhole. None of its walls faced the outside.

No window. No exit except for the door into the hallway.

Claustrophobic. The word flashed through her mind. Nausea threatened to grip her.

Stop it, she exhorted herself. Get on with what you came for.

She gripped the sink hard with both hands and stared down the anxious face in the mirror. It worked. Letting go of the cold porcelain, she muttered softly, "Right, here we go."

Cautious to prevent any squeaking, she inched the mirrored medicine cabinet open. The popping of the magnetic snap-lock sounded startlingly loud. Belatedly, she sought to cover it with a throat-clearing cough.

Ignoring the jumble of cosmetics and assorted medicines, she pointed the flash at the top shelf. No Seconal vial in sight. Her other hand rummaged among bottles and plastic containers on the lower shelves. Theresa's prescription sedative was gone.

Did Theresa store it somewhere safe after she'd sent Agnes to fetch two tablets for Leo? Or did one of the others swipe the container? Everyone had free access to it via the backstair entrance. Plus, several of them, including Leo, entered the private quarters to fetch the blankets.

If someone slipped Leo an additional and perhaps larger dose of the sedative, it would explain why he didn't fight for his life when dunked in the tub.

Weren't some tranquilizers laced with an additive to induce vomiting when overdosed? She dimly recalled reading about it. Which would explain his chucking up.

One thing for sure, even complete disorientation in the wake of an overdose wouldn't account for Leo's entire body ending up lengthwise in the pukey water. The built-in tub at the far end of the upstairs bath only had one broadside not enclosed by walls. He'd keel over head-on, half in, half out of the tub.

At least, that was what logic and practical reason suggested. A forensic team, she figured, might come to a different conclusion. Until such time, she must be on her guard against a killer on the premises. Knowledge, she felt, was the best protection against the unpredictable.

Right, she encouraged herself, let's find out.

Resolved, she eased the cabinet shut and gave her mirror image a thumb-up. No longer concerned about noise, she opened the bathroom door.

A sliver of light from a narrow gap in Theresa's bedsit doorway felt like a beacon in the darkness of the musty corridor. Agnes lifted the flashlight she'd held against her pants leg and aimed it right and left. Too weak to reach the far ends. She simply had to assume no one followed them.

Agnes cleared her throat to forewarn her hostess and called softly, "Theresa? Mind if I come in for a minute?"

She tapped her fingertips against the door. It yielded under the minimal pressure and swung inward. Well-oiled hinges, she deduced.

The room appeared empty. Or, at least, no sign of its owner.

Snug as a bug. Theresa's description of her lair echoed in Agnes's mind. Crammed full was her own assessment. In pride of place sat a queen-size Murphy's bed, fully extended at present and adorned with lacy bedding, countless pillows, and a colorful quilt. A chunky wardrobe, a tallboy, dressers, vanity, and assorted nestling tables loaded with knick-knacks, recognizable in the flickering glimmer from battery-operated tea lights, crowded the room. A voluminous recliner faced the curtained window.

No need to shine the light along the walls. From her previous visit, Agnes recalled a vast assortment of mismatched framed pictures. Most of them were the kind you pick up at jumble sales or receive as gifts from well-meaning acquaintances ignorant of your taste.

A snorting breath alerted Agnes. Of two minds whether to disturb her hostess or leave quietly, she gingerly approached the recliner. Just a peek to make sure Theresa was okay.

Level now with the overstuffed recliner's armrest, she peered down at the tousled, graying curls, illuminated by the dim glow of several tea lights on a side table. Still, she could see the woman's ample bosom heave. The stubby legs in their pale pink sweats twitched once, prompting the feet in furry slippers to bob in reflex on the recliner's footrest.

About to leave her hostess in a much-deserved slumber, Agnes inched backward. Her leg brushed against an occasional table and dislodged some ceramic ornament that clinked sharply on the glass surface.

The sleeper's head jerked forward with a spluttering snort. A wet "What?" and the dimpled hands clutched the armrest as if to heave herself up with the next breath.

"Oh, I'm so sorry. Theresa. It's me, Agnes." She stepped forward to be in full view. "Didn't mean to wake you."

Eyes not quite focused and the voice still somnolent, the dazed lady mumbled, "Goodness, no. Wasn't asleep, dear."

Agnes suppressed a smile. "Sorry. My mistake. It's been such a long night any of us might doze off."

"Never had a night like this." Theresa rubbed her eyes with the back of her hand. "Makes a body right jumpy. Folks get testy when they're tired, don't they? Mind, I'm not complaining."

"You've got every right to complain, Theresa. There you take in uninvited guests and end up with a nightmare. A hurricane is bad enough, but a death in your B&B is horrific." To give her hostess time to recover her senses, she babbled on, "Let's hope Carmen changes her mind about leaving at first light. Not fair to make you deal with formalities." A euphemism if there ever was one, Agnes told herself.

Wriggling upright in her chair, Theresa groped for the footrest lever. A metallic snap and the force of the spring release propelled the chubby woman forward like a pilot ejected by her seat. Theresa's foot, clad in a hand-knitted sock, fished for a wayward slipper, dislodged by the rude awakening.

"Never hold up travelers, is what I say."

Her hostess's unexpected change of heart about Carmen's departure and the prospect of dealing with Leo's remains astonished Agnes.

In case Theresa felt duty bound to check on her guests and thus abort any opportunity for a private chat, Agnes said somewhat fatuously, "Ah, so good having a quiet moment with you. Mind if I sit down?"

Without delay, she grabbed the faux fur stool from the mirrored vanity table and plonked down with her back to the window, facing the older woman squarely.

"I meant to ask you, how are we to contact the police with phone and internet services down? Kieran thinks it'll take a while until they get restored. And the driveway is impassable, he says."

For a moment, Theresa appeared lost for words. Then she beamed. "There's always Farmer Joe."

"Oh? Isn't he in the same boat? I mean, how to reach him, or he get help?" Agnes recalled Theresa mentioning the man had a generator. What good would that do?

"Joe's real handy," her hostess said with conviction. "He's got a vehicle that goes anywhere."

"You mean an ATV? Is there a police detachment close by?" Agnes frowned. "But how can we contact this Joe?"

Theresa chuckled. "Shank's pony."

"What? Riding's not my thing." Agnes felt appalled at the thought. "You don't have—"

"It's an expression." A delighted chortle shook the loose folds of the woman's chins. "My granny's favorite. Means 'on foot.'" Still beaming, she added, "Bet Kieran won't mind. Come to think of it, must be about where their truck broke down. Joe can tow it for them."

Relieved help was near, Agnes nodded. "Sounds good to me." One problem less. On to the next issue while she had her hostess's attention.

"Just wondering. If Carmen really takes off, you've got their ID info and home address from their first visit, don't you? The police will need it."

No immediate answer came. She watched the stubby fingers pick at the doilies spread on the well-worn armrests. An embarrassed expression pinched the lips, and the older woman avoided her questioning gaze.

"Didn't get around to the forms. Poor dears were that tired and hungry. Mind, ten at night it was." It sounded rushed and flustered.

"They showed you ID, though?" Considering the fuss Carmen made about the cousins' IDs, Agnes expected she'd wave hers upon arrival.

"Good grief," cried Theresa, as if vastly surprised. "I forgot to ask. So awkward bothering people. Doubt other B&Bs hold with that, either." The chubby features quivered. "We're not like motels with reception desks and staff, you know."

"I don't blame you, Theresa. Not at all." Agnes didn't recall Theresa requesting any info, not even a home address when she arrived. With her few belongings in storage in Ontario, she'd have been hard-pressed to provide an address. Yet, this was different. Theresa was friends with her mom, Sera.

In an upbeat tone, she said, "We'll just make sure Carmen leaves

Leo's ID and address. Even if she doesn't know his family, the cops won't have trouble tracing them. Bracebridge is a small town."

Oddly, this seemed to increase Theresa's discomfort. Knuckles showed as her hands clutched the chair arms. Agnes noticed the tremor when the grip loosened, and the hands grabbled at the gray curls instead.

"What is it, Theresa? If you want, I can ask Carmen for Leo's ID. You don't have to put up with the woman's abrasive ways."

Or was Theresa now worried about the police questioning her nonchalant business practices? Skipping registration forms smacked of tax fiddle.

"It's not that," Theresa murmured but didn't expand. As if to avoid scrutiny, she turned sideways and reached for matches. The process of lighting the candles in a three-armed candelabra that throned among the bric-à-brac required undue attention.

"This whole situation must be so stressful for you, Theresa." Nightmarish was nearer to the point, Agnes thought, but plowed on. "I'm sure the police will take care of things and arrange for the body's removal." Won't mean 'end of story.' If her intuition proved right, the B&B would become the center of a murder investigation. Did Theresa realize that?

"I'll be glad when they take him away." Theresa heaved a sigh, then went on, "Throws a spanner in my renovation plans, it does. Bathroom comes first now. Folks don't enjoy a bubble bath in a tub where a fellow died, do they?"

A bout of her hostess's tongue clicking gave Agnes a moment to compose her face.

"They won't," she agreed dryly.

The homely woman leaned forward and patted Agnes's knee. Peering into her face, as people do before imparting a confidence, she whispered, "Don't think me unfeeling, dear. He wasn't a nice young fellow, you know."

"Um. Guess not." Agnes prevaricated. "You've seen him before this visit. He certainly seemed nervy and a little odd yesterday."

"Nasty," Theresa said with a decisive nod.

"Oh, I wouldn't say—"

"Raked up the old story, he did. But I set him straight. Wouldn't get a cent out of me. Never mind social media."

Unsure what to make of this, yet sensing its importance, Agnes felt her way cautiously. "I'm sorry to hear that. So tough on you. Raking up the past."

"Your mom told you about my troubles. And me thinking it all forgotten." She leaned forward again. "Don't you believe it, dear. A death haunts you to your grave."

"Yikes, I hope not," Agnes mumbled, completely at sea now.

"Gave me such a turn when Dougie mentioned food poisoning." Dismay flickered in the pale blue eyes.

"Wasn't it Leo, you said? I understood he asked for money." In short, blackmail, she added silently.

"That he did. Nasty lout."

A gulf apart from the poor lamb appellation, Agnes reflected. How get to the bottom of it? Food poisoning. An old story. Hence, predating this B&B. Her mom shared nothing about Theresa other than that she'd known her a long time.

To admit ignorance would probably end the conversation. So, Agnes said vaguely, "Ah, of course. You'd better refresh my memory. Can't exactly recall…"

"Not much to say." Theresa sighed deeply. "People will talk. Small towns have long memories. Folks up in Bracebridge remember. Mind you, the diner is busy as ever. Fellow who bought it from me got lucky. A little goldmine. Went for a song."

A tear rolled down the flabby cheek. It glistened in the candlelight and made its way into the folds of the chin.

"You were forced to sell, weren't you?" Still swimming in murky uncertainty, Agnes latched on to a solid fact.

"What else could I do? The woman was dead, and people stopped coming. Business went down the river in a handbasket." Distress quavered in the plaintive voice.

"My God, how terrible for you," Agnes said with feeling. She could guess now but needed the facts. "A clear case of food poisoning, was it? And they blamed you."

Maybe her gaze was too intense. The older woman's lids squeezed shut, and her right hand shot up to cover the trembling mouth. The fingertips dug into the cheek.

Agnes had to lean in to hear when Theresa muttered, "I told the cops it was just once. Fish looked fresh and nothing wrong with it."

"Yikes, fish poisoning," Agnes prompted. Well, one case was plenty in any dining establishment, she figured.

"Nothing suspicious about the man. Came around by the back door to the kitchen. Fresh catch, he said. Stupid me believed him."

Her hostess's gaze pleaded with Agnes. "Believe me, I've learned my lesson." In a firm tone, she professed, "Never cut corners."

Except in selective bookkeeping, Agnes's mind supplied. Yet she nodded, anyway.

"Did they fine you?" she asked. "Or worse?"

"That they did. Food inspector turned my kitchen upside down." Animated perhaps by the recollected outrage, Theresa wriggled in her seat. "Took samples from the chest freezers. Like I was serving road-kill. The nerve! Nothing doing, I told him. Bet he wanted to close me down for good."

"What a terrible experience," Agnes said. "Of course, the death of a customer is most horrible. It must weigh heavy on your mind." Though she doubted Theresa's mind worked like other people's.

"One hates to speak ill of the dead," Theresa confided. "Between you and me, dear, old Mrs. Hubbard wasn't a nice lady. Always complained we wouldn't allow her dog in. It's against bylaws."

Sounded like Mother Hubbard of the nursery rhyme, Agnes thought. "Yeah, only service dogs permitted."

"The old biddy harassed my staff something fearful." Theresa resumed her tale. "Special orders. My, you couldn't please the woman. No one could."

Connecting the threads, Agnes asked, "So, Leo heard about it? How long ago was it? Was he still a kid back then?" Strange he'd remember.

"Going on five years now. The high school kids would pop in for takeouts or a quick lunch. And hung out after school. We had a nice bar counter for sundaes and burgers. Real popular it was." Nostalgic pride rang in her voice. "Like the 50s I decorated that section, movie posters, vinyl galore, the whole hog."

"Did Leo recognize you right away?"

"That I couldn't say. Not a word the other day."

Agnes' sleep deprived brain tried to recapture her impression of Leo from the previous evening, which seemed ages ago. Instead, an image of Theresa's agitation last night resurfaced. Now, it made sense.

To make sure, she said, "When you went to fetch blankets, Leo followed you. That's when he badgered you."

A wary flicker narrowed Theresa's eyes. Her tone suspicious, she asked, "Did he tell you?"

"No. Of course not. A mere guess. It took far longer than it would take for blankets. Carmen got impatient and went to check. You were alone with him for quite a while and seemed upset when you returned."

Like a deflated balloon, her hostess's ample torso collapsed in a huge sigh. "Thank heaven for small mercies. Got me worried for a moment. Thought he went around telling people."

"Well, unlikely he'd tell me," Agnes said. "Never got a chance to chat with him." It triggered another memory. "As far as I know, the only one he talked to was Carmen. And Doug. I saw them together."

"Goodness! That explains things." Agitated, Theresa scuttled to the edge of the recliner's floppy seat. Dark patches rose to her cheeks.

"What do you mean?"

"Why, of course, him harping on food poisoning. Gave me such a turn, Dougie did. Such a nice family man, too."

Helplessly, Agnes watched Theresa's mouth chatter in the grip of a powerful emotion.

"Might be coincidence," she said soothingly. "With the fridge off for hours and talk of food spoiling easily, naturally the topic came to mind."

Theresa wasn't listening. Hands clasped to her bosom, she muttered, "And me thinking I was safe now. It'll haunt me to my grave. That it will."

Chapter 17

Her hostess's dire, yet ambiguous, prophecy of being haunted to the grave sent shivers down Agnes's arms.

"It's cold in here, isn't it?" Theresa eyed her with concern.

"I'm okay." Agnes didn't correct the misconception and tugged her fleece jacket close to feel its comforting embrace.

"Time I get back to my guests," Theresa said and blew out the candles. With a groan, she struggled to her feet, hampered by stubby legs and a tilting jumbo size chair. "Mind, Agnes," she raised a warning finger, "not a word to anyone about our little chat."

"Understood." She helped Theresa flip the tea lights to extinguish them.

At the door, awareness dawned. "Is it just me, or is it quieter in here?" Now that she focused on the sound, a mere sustained whooshing was audible. Yet, the bedsit's windows were on the same side as the backdoor where the spruce crashed earlier.

The older woman stood still, one hand cupping her ear. "Storm's dying down."

Agnes would have liked to peek out the window to confirm the prognosis, but her hostess shooed her into the corridor, saying, "Go ahead, dear. I'll just freshen up a bit and be right with you."

When Agnes entered the living room, she first thought no one was there. Someone must have extinguished the oil lamp and most candles. A murky dimness prevailed.

Then she noticed a flickering on the far side. Her flashlight weakly illuminated two figures bent over a tiny table, their heads almost touching.

Their faces turned toward the light as the beam and the sound of the closing door alerted them, and Agnes saw it was Kieran and Rob. They huddled together, too immersed in whatever they were doing to acknowledge her return. The flickering came from a votive candle burned low in a glass holder on their little table.

The door behind her opened, and Agnes stepped aside to let Theresa pass.

Rob called as if caught in a naughty act, "Do you mind, ma'am? We saw the shelf with the games and stuff and borrowed your chess."

Their hostess chuckled affably. "You're most welcome. Games are free for all." She waddled into the room. "Why sit in the dark? The oil lamp ran dry, I bet. Gets a refill in a jiffy."

"Might not need it," Kieran said. "I snuffed it, as no one needed light."

"My, you're a cautious one." Theresa chuckled. "Better safe than sorry. I'll be in the kitchen. Holler if you need me."

"Want some help?" Agnes asked.

"Thanks, dear. There's nothing for you to do but to have a little snooze on the sofa."

"Sure will," Agnes said but walked over to the nearest window.

Up close, the whooshing increased, but nowhere near the horrific frenzy of an hour or two ago. She lifted the heavy curtain and found the window less obstructed by shredded leaf matter. To shut out the reflection from candles Theresa was relighting, Agnes stepped behind the drapery and pressed her face close to the glass. Its coolness felt refreshing.

Once her eyes adjusted and she'd wiped away her breath's condensation with her sleeve, she could make out shapes in the murky grayness of pre-dawn.

Everything was in motion out there, whipping back and forth. Was that the giant poplar in the drive bent low? For an instant, it straightened, only to bow again as in a curtsey to Tempesta, the Roman goddess of storms.

Fanciful again. She smiled to herself.

The curtain lifted of its own accord, or so it seemed.

"See anything?" asked Kieran's voice above her head.

"Barely just. Have a look." She moved over to make room. "The glass is not as coated on this side."

With the two of them encapsulated by draperies, it felt unexpectedly intimate. Under different circumstances—

Oh, quit it, her sterner self ordered, impatiently stifling the budding thought.

Unaware of the effect his presence had, or so she assumed, Kieran mumbled, "Thanks," and peered out, his forehead leaning against the pane.

"Slowing down a bit," he said. "Give it a couple hours."

"Still potent enough to flatten that poplar," Agnes remarked. Was she trying to impress him with arborist lore? Tell a poplar from a spruce? she thought wryly.

"They shoot up high. Too skinny for their own good," he said. "Wind's over 50. They can't take it."

"Kilometers per hour?"

"Yeah, no. Miles. And gusting."

As if by mutual consent, they turned to leave their cozy confinement. Kieran lifted the curtain for her to pass.

The room seemed bright enough to make her blink. Theresa had cranked the oil lamp at the center of the harvest table to a stronger flame.

Something glittering in her peripheral vision drew Agnes's attention to the staircase. It was light bouncing off Doug's spectacles. The man's smallish figure almost disappeared in a voluminous wing chair tucked in a nook by the stairs. Had he been there all along? A silent observer?

Two fingers reached for his glasses and removed them by the hinge of the arm. His other hand withdrew a miniature chamois from his pocket. Lips forming an O, he breathed on the lenses and proceeded to polish them.

The operation seemed to require his full concentration. Yet Agnes felt certain he was observing her keenly.

Uncomfortable under the scrutiny, she pivoted toward the cousins at the opposite end of the room. They'd resumed their game.

She strolled over and said, "Theresa told me about a farmer with an ATV. Lives up the road. He might get in touch with the police if the phone service is still down in the morning."

"Ach aye," said Kieran. "That'll be grand."

"Joe can tow your truck," Theresa called from the kitchen.

Must have owl ears, Agnes thought. They hadn't spoken loudly.

The older woman bustled over, saying, "Joe's just a stone's throw away. Bit over half a mile west. Bet your truck's smack in front of his place."

"Could be," said Kieran.

"Me or Kieran can head out at sunup," Rob said. "Us think we have a go with the chainsaw when it's light."

"Want proper light for that," agreed the tall cousin. "No messing with a blade in the dark."

"Good grief!" cried Theresa. "Too dangerous by half. We waited this long. A few hours more won't matter."

"Absolutely right, dear Mrs. Mae." Doug must have listened in. Now, he nodded his approval.

"Dougie! My, I didn't see you in the old grandfather chair." Theresa ambled over to him. "Can I get you anything?"

"Thank you kindly, dear lady," came his stock reply. "I'll just sit here quietly and have a little snooze."

"If you say so." Their hostess sounded disappointed but withdrew to the kitchen.

For the life of her, Agnes couldn't figure out the dynamics between that pair. From Theresa's private comments, she inferred the woman feared Doug had ferreted out the secret of her Bracebridge past. Was Theresa's Dougie'ing a means of prejudicing him in her favor? If so, it was ill-chosen. Subtle clues showed the man disliked the ridiculous diminutive.

Well, not her problem, Agnes figured, and curled up on the sofa, literally turning her back on the man.

She felt buoyed by the prospect of morning and help mere hours away. Even if the sun dawned on another rainy day, the hurricane would be well on its offshore way. Hopefully, veering toward the open Atlantic rather than heading north, wreaking havoc in Newfoundland.

Idly, she watched the cousins at their game. Heads bent close again. They sat across from each other, separated by the low occasional table, its top the size of the chessboard. If they talked at all, it must be via telepathy. They seemed perfectly content to await daylight.

Carmen's fancy about them being the convenience store robbers and Leo's killers was ludicrous. The cousins had nothing to hide. Ordinary guys, Agnes felt convinced. And helpful. Unlike some others.

Her lids drooped as if to close the topic. But shutting out the light brought on darker thoughts. No matter how much she tried to evade the truth, it obtruded relentlessly.

If someone here had a whopping motive to get rid of Leo, it was motherly Theresa. Blackmail posed a nasty threat. If Leo had lived even another day, he might have wreaked irreparable damage to Theresa's business venture. Start a social media smear campaign and thrash out the food poisoning death story, splash it all over online reviews, and Theresa's B&B baby would die in its infancy.

Agnes sighed. Her hostess probably invested every penny salvaged from the Bracebridge diner. This place might be mortgaged to the hilt to finance renovations. To envision all she'd built after the Ontario fiasco go down the drain might prompt desperate action.

Plus, it was Theresa who offered the tranquilizers. Did she slip Leo the vial? So easy if he asked for more when the two were alone. Plied him with the cure-all brandy?

Didn't Leo hit on Doug for booze? Alone with Theresa while rounding up blankets, he'd plenty of opportunity to cage a few drinks. Then sprang the blackmail scheme on the hapless woman.

Dazed and doped as he was, it would be easy to dunk Leo in the tub if Theresa later surprised him chucking up in the bathroom. Flip him over the rim. Hold him under and away you go. Didn't require much strength. Blackmail problem solved.

At the thought, Agnes snapped wide awake. She wriggled into a sitting position and peeked over the back of the sofa. Unaware of being cast in the role of a murderess, the woman swept the kitchen with a broom, a frilly apron in shocking pink tied around the bulging middle.

Could this warm-hearted lady, who took in stranded strangers, kill? The notion seemed even more ludicrous than casting the cousins, of whom Agnes knew nothing, as killers.

Yet a nagging memory remained. When they talked, Agnes sensed no compassion at the death of old Mrs. Hubbard. Serving fish obtained from dubious sources alone was culpable. If Theresa got away with merely a fine, the law must have accepted extenuating circumstances. Or Theresa was cleverer in covering her tracks than she let Agnes believe.

Still, to resort to murder in safeguarding the business would be downright lunacy. The savvy B&B proprietress must realize others might recognize her.

Tourism on PEI drew primarily on visitors from Ontario and Quebec. Hence, the chances of someone from Bracebridge or a Muskoka area cottager happening by, even if slim, weren't negligible. Hard to believe anyone would kill to keep the story under wraps.

What's more, Theresa must assume Leo gabbed to Carmen. Though, come to think of it, the young woman gave no sign of being in the blackmail loop.

Could Theresa be sure of that? It defeated credulity to imagine the broom-wielding pink lady to have murder on her mind. Plotting to eliminate Leo.

Yeah, right. Absurd, like a penny thriller, Agnes's mind scoffed.

Another thought struck her with full force.

Where was Carmen?

Chapter 18

"Where is Carmen?" Agnes blurted out.

"Eh?" Kieran's head swung around, his expression abstracted as if plotting his next move.

"*En garde*," said Rob, apparently about to take Kieran's queen.

"Bet she's gone upstairs," said Theresa, leaning on her broom.

"A wake or vigil throughout the night was a commonplace practice," Doug remarked. "In Mediterranean countries and in the Near East, folks hire wailing women."

"Is that right? What next?" Theresa rested her chin on the broom head.

Ordinarily, the point might have raised Agnes's zest for discussion. Professional mourning women featured in classic literature. Right now, she couldn't care less.

Impatient with inaction, she slipped off the sofa and grabbed the flashlight.

"I'll pop up to my room," she said.

Theresa nodded. "You do that, dear. Quieter up there."

"Checkmate." Rob sounded smug and looked it too when Agnes glanced in the players' direction.

Kieran frowned at the board, then at Agnes, but withheld comment.

Doug's thin lips stretched into a bland smile when she passed the grandfather chair.

Halfway up, just past the twist in the stairs, she heard the wooden treads creak behind her. She quickened her steps and hurried to the lobby at the top. Once there, she pivoted and pointed her flashlight downward. The beam reflected on her follower's lenses.

"Coming up, too?" she asked redundantly and lowered the beam to catch on his shiny shoes.

One hand clutching the railing, the odd fellow ascended, all the while nodding in little spurts.

Agnes didn't wait but proceeded into the upper corridor.

The man's mincing gait must make for surprising speed because, in no time, he caught up with her. Nor did he stop when they passed his door.

She was just about to ask him where he was headed when she saw Carmen.

"Drat the woman," Agnes muttered.

"That's your room," Doug said, keeping his voice low. "Didn't you lock it?"

"Shoot. Thought I…" Agnes mumbled. "Oh, well. It's okay."

When they drew level, the imposing six-footer-plus loomed over them. The woman's hand still rested on Agnes's doorknob with a proprietorial air.

Doug switched on his LED torch but directed the beam at the floor.

Maybe Agnes's expression gave her away.

For Carmen drawled, "Something wrong?" Her tone grew aggressive. "You told me I could."

"Um, yes. Didn't expect you'd use it in my absence, I guess."

"Duh? Like in grade school? *Mi-iss?* Can I use the washroom?" Her imitation of a first grader was perfect.

"Never mind." Agnes's impatience got the better of her. "It's only for a few more hours." Then she changed tack. "Are you still planning on leaving at daybreak?"

"Yeah? So what?" Carmen's narrowed eyes challenged her.

"Nothing. Just wondering." Pointless to tell the woman how unfair and even outrageous it was to expect Theresa to deal with the aftermath of Leo's death. Except if their hostess caused Leo's demise.

Carmen glared at Agnes, treating Doug like a fly on the wall. With her trademark "Whatever," she swung around and swaggered toward the backstairs.

Bemused, Agnes watched her go. Part of her mind puzzled about Doug's continued presence. The man hadn't said a word.

Unsure how to get rid of him, she said, "Good of you to walk me to my door."

"Not at all." He neither moved nor reacted to the mild sarcasm.

Still staring at the door to the backstairs after it snapped into its lock, realization dawned. Someone had pulled the drapes of the window at the far end. Diffused gray light penetrated through the diagonal streak free of vegetation debris.

Intrigued, Agnes went to glance out.

Close up, she could distinguish tree shapes bending in the wind. Her downward glance, with her nose pressed to the glass, spied the massive body of the toppled spruce. If such a giant fell victim to the hurricane, what horror-scape awaited them in full daylight?

She shuddered at the thought.

"Young Ms. Carmen can't leave by the backdoor."

Douglas Junior's voice startled Agnes. She hadn't noticed him following her to the window. His torch was switched off. How could the man tread so softly in his patent leather Oxfords?

Irritated, she said, "I realize that. I expect she prefers the backstairs as closest to her room." Her hand automatically pointed at the room across from the double-doored linen closet.

"I fear you are mistaken." The odious man raised a finger as if to scold. "Ms. Carmen's room is across from your own."

"Eh? But I thought that's where Theresa put the cousins. I mean Kieran and Rob. No?" Her voice petered out.

Douglas Junior's eyes blinked rapidly. "Did you, now? The young men occupy this room."

Stunned, Agnes stared at him. "Are you sure?"

Before her eyes, the mildly ridiculous gent morphed again into an alert observer.

"Absolutely," he said. "Now, why would this upset you, I wonder?"

Her mind registered the words but refused to listen. "But—but the balaclava," she muttered.

"Which balaclava might that be?" Doug asked softly.

Her stare shifted to his bland features. Irrelevantly, she noticed the lenses didn't magnify his eyes. Must be a weak prescription. Like window glass. Were the steel-rimmed spectacles a vanity? Didn't improve his looks. Perhaps a prop.

Ignoring his question, she asked, "Where did you find me when I fainted?"

The sharp glance told her he was following her mental perambulation.

"Outside Ms. Carmen's door."

There was nothing for it but to risk becoming explicit. "Was her door open?"

"No. Her door was closed, just like your own."

His steady gaze did not leave her face. They were at eye level, quite the same height. She felt the blood drain from her face. Wanted to escape scrutiny. Think this out by herself.

Like leaches, the pupils didn't let her go.

He took a step toward her. "Are you all right? Do you feel faint?" His hand reached as if to steady her.

Agnes drew back and bumped against the wall.

"It's nothing. Just remembered something," she mumbled vaguely.

Wrong thing to say.

He pounced on it. "You remember who hit you? Don't you?"

"Um, no. Of course not," she stammered. "How could I? Didn't see anyone."

"But an educated guess," he insisted, abandoning the ineffectual geezer sham. "You thought it was this Kieran, and now you realize the giant Carmen would fit the bill. A veritable Valkyrie, our Ms. Carmen."

Still watching her closely, he added in conversational tones, "In mythology, the Valkyries guide the souls of the dead to Valhalla."

This extraneous point allowed her to recover. Straightening, she said, "I thought no such thing of Kieran. He seems a decent fellow."

"The redoubtable Ms. Carmen disagrees. We both heard her accuse the young men." His penetrating gaze sought to pin her like a butterfly. "They drowned her boyfriend in the bathwater. Or so she claimed."

Agnes's hand flew up. It took willpower to prevent it from shielding her eyes to evade his stare. Slowly, she stroked her cheek as if in thought.

The touch calmed her. Deliberately pacing the words, she said, "You're not a father of five, are you? It's an act you put on. Self-effacing at will."

A deep frown contracted his forehead up to the balding pate. "Wherever did that come from?" Suddenly, he sounded like a normal guy.

"Oh, skepticism is a professional hazard of philosophy profs," she said airily. "At times, the role seemed to slip. Makes one think. Some sort of undercover job for the government? An inspector? A tax collector?"

At her half-hearted jest, Douglas Junior stepped back, the features expressionless.

"A dangerous assumption, don't you think?" His voice was silky soft. "It's the last thing one would want someone to uncover—pardon the pun."

Not a denial, rather a warning, Agnes supposed. Or a command not to out him? Get real, she thought. Who's fooling whom, here?

"Mum's the word." She nodded in mock solemnity. "Your secret is safe with me."

His lips twitched in ironic acknowledgment.

The thought of having a potential ally in this madhouse buoyed her. Still, caution was the better part of wisdom.

Her gaze fastened on the door through which Carmen departed minutes ago. Bits and pieces of the night's events flooded her mind. Half-understood words and observations crowded in.

"It can't be," she mumbled and involuntarily peered over her shoulder at the door to Leo's deathbed.

"That the woman drowned her boyfriend? Drowned him like a rat?" Doug's words uncannily expressed her brain's wild conjectures.

She shot him a grateful half-smile. Playing for time, she asked, "Is that what you believe?"

"My dear young lady," he said, slipping back into his former role. "I am trying to divine your train of thought. You are not the most forthright woman."

A snort escaped her. "You're the one to talk, my dear Father-of-Five," she mimicked his absurd mannerism.

"What may I ask makes you question my fatherhood of five healthy children?" He sounded curious rather than offended.

"Um, you just don't look it. Or perhaps you're trying too hard." She shrugged, unable to pinpoint her doubts.

"I see."

What he saw remained unstated. Instead, he reverted to the pertinent issue. "As you have cast me in the role of a gumshoe, why not run your logical deductions by me? I don't lay claim to criminal expertise but may serve as a solid sounding board."

When she still hesitated, he said with an indulgent smile, "You don't trust me, do you? Or do you want the sleuthing honor all to yourself?"

Stung, she burst into speech. "I'm no sleuth. Or, at least, never willingly," she added for honesty's sake. After all, she had a case or two under her belt.

"Then let's hear your theory." He switched on his torch and, tucking it in under his arm to illuminate the floor, leaned against the opposite wall like settling in for a cozy chat.

"Give me a moment to collect my thoughts," she said and received a nod.

Was it safe to talk? Here? In the dimly lit corridor? Late in the day for scruples, Agnes's mind scoffed.

At least, the man himself appeared to be safe. If indeed working undercover, he might be a useful ally. Or, if really an ordinary family man, innocently caught up in this situation like she was, there was no harm in sharing. He might roll his eyes at her wild surmises. So what?

Either way, unlike the others below, Douglas Junior had no motive to eliminate the unfortunate Leo.

Even if, by some freak chance, the dapper fellow was some homicidal maniac who offed unsuspecting young men, sharing her suspicions about Carmen would deflect his attention from herself.

If she was right and Carmen was the killer, then the woman must not be allowed to escape. Alone, Agnes couldn't stop her. Okay, Doug wasn't Superman, either. Yet, if he too believed Carmen to be the perpetrator, then the cousins were innocent, and she could enlist their help.

Though it took her feverish brain only moments to reach this conclusion, her eyes had lost focus. She snapped into awareness of the man opposite. Doug regarded her with calm inquiry, biding his time.

Disconcerted by his steady gaze, she said, "Er, not sure this is a good place."

"There's no one up here," he said. "This corner suits the purpose. The emergency exit is made of steel. Virtually soundproof as far as eavesdropping goes."

"Right," she said. "Here goes."

Chapter 19

Agnes took another deep breath to fortify herself before risking full disclosure.

"It's true. Carmen wanted us to believe Rob killed Leo. Given what she'd insinuated earlier, not that farfetched," Agnes said, rueful about falling for the ruse.

Doug raised a questioning eyebrow, and Agnes hastened on, "She hinted the cousins were the convenience store robbers."

Both brows now shot up. The movement dislodged the carefully pasted strands from the pate in the most disconcerting way.

"A rather outlandish idea," he commented. A mischievous glimmer wrinkled the corners of his eyes, or so it seemed when he moved the torch to switch it off.

"Yeah, I know." In defense of her own gullibility, Agnes reasoned, "Those robbers must sleep somewhere tonight. A B&B is a viable option."

"True." He regarded her shrewdly. "But you no longer believe that?"

"Oh, I do. Just not that it's the cousins."

The man chuckled. Did he find her laughable?

Fingers drumming his chest, he mocked, "You are not suggesting that I am the elusive villain?"

"No, of course not. I think Carmen and Leo robbed the store. One of them shot the man."

Doug's face sobered. "The news spoke of two men. Ms. Carmen is not a man."

"They said a tall and a shorter one. That fits. You didn't see them arrive. In a hooded jacket, Carmen passes off as a male. Add a bala-clava, and you couldn't tell the difference." That got his attention. "Besides," she continued, "a witness might be too upset to look closely."

"I see." He sounded thoughtful. After a moment's reflection, he said, "I assumed you believed a lover's quarrel was young Leo's undo-ing. Not excusable, but understandable if Ms. Carmen lost her patience with the childish boy."

"You mean because Leo whined and pestered people?" Agnes remembered well Doug's annoyance at the unwanted follower. "Sure, he bugged you and got on Carmen's nerves. Still, I doubt that got him killed."

Better not mention how much Leo bothered Theresa. Blackmail was too serious and yielded a potent motive. If Doug had ferreted out their hostess's past, he'd jump to that conclusion.

Hard to read the man's reaction. The yellow glow of her flashlight reflected on the spectacles and hid his expression.

His tongue clucking showed him unconvinced. So did the pedantic tone when he pointed out, "It would take excessive exposure for such unpleasant behavior to result in murder."

"Of course it would. I wasn't suggesting you or Rob, for that matter, dunked the poor kid because you were fed up with him."

He huffed and muttered, "I should hope not."

Why was he harping on this, anyway? she thought. Did he feel pestered by his own kids? If he was away a lot, they understandably might demand attention when he got home.

"The way I figure it," Agnes went on, "Carmen worried about Leo going to pieces and inadvertently betraying their secret. A nervy guy isn't an ideal partner in crime."

Her choice of words reminded Agnes of Carmen's overreaction when she'd referred to Leo as a partner.

"Hm, yes." Doug nodded. "There's something to that."

"Perhaps Leo dropped the balaclava in the hallway, and his carelessness alarmed Carmen." As she spoke, Agnes felt her eyes widen. Her mind recalled the image of the silvery doorknob poking the black fabric like wooly lips.

Had she sealed Leo's fate by drawing his partner's attention to his criminal ineptitude?

"If they were robbers, such negligence would be worrying. Murder seems a drastic remedy," he said mildly.

Was he playing devil's advocate? Agnes wondered. Fine with her.

"Granted. Carmen tried to sedate him," she said. "Shut him up for tonight. Since he roamed the hallway, it obviously didn't work. Remember, I saw him hit on you for booze. Carmen couldn't be sure what he'd try next."

Again, she felt Doug's gaze as if he wanted to dissect her brain. Yet, he held his peace. Something about her own words didn't sit right. Vaguely, she added, "She might have followed him into the bathroom, and they argued."

"And he accidentally drowned when she pushed him around?" Doug asked. "Why insist on murder?"

"No," Agnes said. "Not accidentally. The way the tub's built into the window nook of the room, someone must have flung him in deliberately. Or flipped his legs over if Leo leaned into the tub, chucking up. He couldn't end up lengthwise, face-down, by accident. Someone held him under, or he'd have crawled out."

Her lengthy, fast-spoken explanation left her somewhat breathless. When no response came, she admitted, "My reasoning might be counter-factual. Forensics will prove or disprove it."

His slow nod seemed to clinch it. He took her seriously.

She let out a deep breath that turned into a groan. "Jeez, I can't wait for this night to end and the police to take over. What a nightmare. Especially for Theresa."

Doug allowed himself a tiny grin if the thinning lips signified that. "Mrs. Mae," he said drily, "appears to take it in her usual manner."

Whatever that meant, Agnes thought. Was he capable of sarcasm? She rode to their hostess's defense. "Poor Theresa. It would be awful if Carmen escaped."

"You mean and leave our good landlady holding the can? If you permit the colloquialism." With a fastidious expression, he wrinkled his nose, like sensing a foul odor.

"Oh, stop play-acting with me," she burst out. Then mildly, "Theresa's very kind and generous. She'd worked hard to make a go of this place. I'd hate to have an investigation interfere."

Last thing Theresa needed was for anyone to revive the fatal Bracebridge episode. Questioned closely by the police, as was bound to happen once they investigated Leo's death, Theresa might inadvertently blab about the blackmail. Thus, serving a whopping motive on a platter.

Agnes sighed, exasperated at her own inadequacy. "If only there was conclusive proof I could present to the police instead of unsupported surmises."

Douglas Junior's index finger rose to tap the side of his nose.

"What is it?" she asked. Was he being cute?

"I wonder," he said ponderously. "When Ms. Carmen knocked you over the noggin—We can assume it was she. Can't we?" Agnes nodded, and he went on, "You were searching her room, I take it?"

"Er, yes and no. You see, at the time, I took it for the cousins' room. Plus, she floored me before I could search."

"What did you hope to find?"

"Evidence, of course. Of the robbery, I mean." Agnes pushed back her hair, embarrassed to admit the vagueness of her quest. "I figured Leo might have found something more conclusive than the balaclava and got killed for his pains."

When she stopped, Doug nodded encouragingly.

So she said, "You'd all gone downstairs. The right time to have a peek at the cousins' duffle bag, I thought." She smiled ruefully. "Got this vague notion of something in the room before blacking out." Her fingers grabbled at her hairline. "No good. I draw a blank."

"Hm. Maybe we can remedy that. Check what you missed."

"Search the room now? I'm sure Carmen wouldn't be so stupid to leave it unlocked. Last time, she'd probably made a quick trip to the loo, and I lucked out finding her door open." The remembered pain made her wince. "Well, luck's the wrong word."

"Just wait in your room, Agnes. Give me a few minutes to fetch Mrs. Mae's master key. Discreetly, of course. We'll soon sort this out."

Though Agnes bristled at his taking charge in a paternal fashion, sending her to her room no less, she acquiesced. His quick thinking was admirable. Theresa must have second keys to all rooms. Why hadn't she thought of that?

"Okay," she said. "I hope Theresa won't alert Carmen inadvertently."

"Trust me. I know what I'm doing."

Famous last words, Agnes thought, as he aimed for the backstairs. In a surprisingly normal gait, she noticed. He must have cat eyes, for he didn't switch on his torch.

Back in her own room, she breathed a sigh of relief. A brief respite to gather her wits was most welcome.

Almost from habit, she padded over to the window. The thick coating did not let light penetrate. They'd need glass scrapers to remove this vegetation goo. Once it dried, it would bake on like a patina. And just as green.

Insignificant worry compared to the immediate concern. What if she'd got it all wrong and Theresa was the culprit, after all? Nonsense, she chided her wayward mind.

If a search of Carmen's room proved inconclusive, her theorizing would go back to square one. For now, her current hypothesis held until disproved.

Agnes lit a candle on the coffee table and switched off the flash, amazed the batteries held out. Huddled in an armchair, she reexamined her line of reasoning.

Assuming Carmen and Leo committed the robbery, then one of them shot the cashier. A grab-and-run Carmen had called it, Agnes remembered now.

If she and Kieran were right about Leo's drug habit, he might be unpredictable, period. Scaredy cat, as Theresa dubbed Leo, might shoot in a panic.

Say Leo panicked during the hold-up. By the time they got to the B&B, Leo had been a basket case who fainted at a loud crash. Was the astraphobia Carmen's invention to cover up for her partner going into a tailspin? Sedating him hadn't worked. He must have seemed a huge liability to Carmen. So, the woman silenced him for good.

Carmen, Agnes assumed, would only kill if it were expedient. With the woman's sense of entitlement and egoism, self-preservation would trump all other considerations. If she shot the cashier, the rest would still hold. Or even more so. A killer had much more to fear than a robber. Either way, Carmen had a compelling motive to kill her loose cannonball of a partner.

The only little problem was how to prove any of this. Agnes closed her eyes and groaned out loud. Why was pinning down criminals so darn difficult?

Because you're not trained for it, a rogue part of her brain jibed. Leave catching killers to the experts.

A soft tapping on her door aborted any attempt at self-justification.

She switched on the flashlight and blew out the candle, releasing a waxy smoke smell.

When she opened her door cautiously, Doug stood dangling a key like a lure.

Chapter 20

Out in the dark hallway, Agnes felt like a cat burglar about to strike. An adrenalin rush set her cheeks aflame. It brought on a memory flash of another nighttime prowl and illicit raid. One that had ended badly—

Don't think of it, she ordered herself. This is different. For one, it's early morning.

The inane comparison restored her sense of proportion. She'd like to believe Doug was an undercover something or other with authority to enter a premise uninvited. Though, didn't they need a warrant unless immediate danger threatened?

The man himself rejoined her noiselessly in the gloomy dimness after checking the lobby to make sure they were alone up here. He'd told her to keep her flash switched off and didn't use his LED.

"Ready?" he murmured.

Cautiously, he unlocked Carmen's room and ushered Agnes inside. When he shut the door with the merest click, panic sent hot waves through Agnes's body.

Her trembling fingers found the rubbery button on her flashlight. As its weakened beam came on, she sucked in her breath noisily. With all her might, she suppressed an urge to flee the scene of attack, if not on her life, but near enough to make no difference in the panic department.

The unmade bed unsettled her for reasons she couldn't comprehend. Quilt and bedding lay bunched in a heap. Sprawled atop were Carmen's discarded gray sweats.

"Where's Carmen?" Agnes whispered.

"Snoozing on the sofa." Doug sounded unconcerned. Was he amused at her anxious tone or at the perp's oblivion to their raid?

The LED lit up and swept the room. Its bright white light reassured Agnes.

"No time to lose," Doug said. "I tackle the wardrobe, and you check the nightstand and dresser."

"Okay." A specific task gave her a sense of purpose.

"Also, check under the pillows," Doug commanded as he opened the armoire's double doors.

Eager that no trace should betray their search, Agnes proceeded with care. She didn't expect Carmen and Leo to have bothered unpacking and storing stuff. Must make sure.

The nightstand's top drawer held nothing but a leaflet advertising the B&B and a bible, whose pristine condition no one might ever disturb. A second drawer contained brochures about PEI's chief attractions.

Agnes shut the drawers and went over to the dresser. It took seconds to confirm it was empty except for lavender-scented liners.

From behind, she heard the wardrobe doors shut with faint clicks.

"Find anything?" she asked.

"Clean as a whistle." He moved on to the desk under the curtained window.

Agnes eyed the bed, ready to lean over its head end to check under the pillows. Then stopped dead.

Memory flooded back. Of course! She'd been reaching for a black shape half-hidden at the foot of the bed before she blacked out.

Excited now, Agnes tore at the strewn bedding. There it was. A fat, elongated something, wrapped now in a sheet to evade immediate detection.

"Found it," she blurted out and was shushed for her troubles.

"Not so loud," Doug whispered. "Let's not draw attention prematurely."

Agnes paid him no heed and seized the sheet. A duffle bag. Impatiently, she unzipped it.

"What have we got here?" he murmured, bending over the side of the bed. His torch pointed right inside the bag. "Careful about fingerprints."

Agnes jerked back like the bag suddenly stood aflame. Her outstretched arms shot back, hugging herself. Hands tucked into her armpits, she whispered, "Okay. You search."

Grunting appreciation, Doug pulled a few tissues from a box on the nightstand and, with their help, removed the contents of the bag, one piece at a time.

With clothes emerged a sour sweat odor from the bag. To judge by the size of the stuff, few items belonged to Leo. In kind and dark coloring, the clothing looked much the same.

Agnes took a moment to check the pillows while waiting. Nothing there. When she turned back, she saw Doug's hands deep in the bag but immobile. A frown clouded his face.

With infinite care, he removed a small, oblong cardboard box.

"Ammo," he muttered.

He grabbed a fresh tissue and eased open the lid. "Almost full."

His hands explored the remaining contents of the bag even more cautiously.

"Gotcha." A grin lit up his bland features as he removed another black garment and slowly unrolled XXL boxer shorts. Inside rested a gun.

Despite expecting such a discovery, Agnes jumped when Doug held the lethal weapon aloft, his fingers clothed by the underwear.

"Oh, my God," she whispered. "She did it."

"Well, not so fast, young woman." The stilted tone resurfaced. "Ballistics would need to match the bullet to the gun. If the bullet was found."

"That's likely, isn't it? They'd find it either in the body or on the scene of crime," said Agnes with a rising sense of elation. What a piece of luck. Knock-down evidence.

Spoilsport Doug blew her bubble, saying, "There might be a second gun."

"All the more reason not to let Carmen escape," Agnes countered. "If there's really another gun, it's in this room. Or she might carry it in her baggy sweats. Or it's in the SUV."

It didn't take long to search the bedding and below the mattress. Under the bed lurked only a few dust bunnies.

"Nothing." Agnes straightened up. "What do we do with this one?" She eyed the ominous weapon that flashed malevolently in the torch's beam. Belatedly, she realized they'd done nothing to record its provenance.

Her hands already patted the pockets of her fleece for her phone. "We need to take pics. Ought to have done right away." She frowned at Doug. Why hadn't he thought of that?

Not waiting for a response, she took a few shots of the gun on the crumpled sheets.

"Give me some light with your torch," she told Doug.

He obliged and made sure it did not reflect on the metal.

"We could reenact you removing it from the undies," she said but retracted immediately. "Nah, that would be cheating."

"Nor would I allow you to take my picture." A little pompous, he added, "My position demands caution."

"Yeah, I guess so." Did he think she'd splash his pic all over social media?

Doug scrutinized the gun and used a wad of tissues to slip it into his cardigan pocket. It bulged noticeably.

Did the thing have a safety catch? Presumably, the man checked, Agnes assumed.

"You go ahead and join the others," he commanded. "I'll follow after storing this safely. It won't do for us to be seen together. Act normally, and don't let on what we found."

"Shouldn't we warn Theresa? Enlist Kieran's help? He's hunky and can handle Carmen." Reckless to have a killer on the loose among unsuspecting people.

"No." His categorical negation brooked no objection.

"What if Carmen does have another gun? We'd put everyone at

risk. Plus, she's huge and fit like a bull." Agnes didn't want to say outright how shrimp-like Doug seemed by comparison.

A twisty smile brushed aside Agnes's concerns. "I'm armed and well capable of dealing with hunks, Carmen or otherwise."

When she still regarded him doubtfully, he said in reassuring tones, "Trust me, Agnes, and keep it under your hat. We both know how our good landlady would react. The McGuinty already dislike Carmen. Any sign we're on to her would spook our perp."

Though Agnes felt reluctant to admit it, Doug had a point. Who knew how Theresa might react? And Kieran would want to tackle Carmen right away. They needed to stall her until the police arrived. Some delay tactics.

With a satisfied glint, Doug switched off his LED and slid toward the door. The glow of her own flash threw murky shadows on the wall. Batteries must run low.

"Turn off your light," he ordered.

Agnes stared at him in panic. "Can't see without—" His contemptuous expression stopped her.

"Only until I've checked the hallway," he explained with exaggerated patience. "You can use it when you're a few steps away. Or if it worries you so much, hop across to your own door and pretend you're just leaving your room."

"Okay. Hurry. This room freaks me out in the dark," Agnes muttered. Easy for him. He didn't get knocked over the head here.

Her stomach lurched painfully when she extinguished the flash. She gripped the metal tube so hard her hand cramped.

A diffuse, grayish streak appeared where she knew the door to be. Doug must have opened it soundlessly. Her eyes readjusted, thankful for the weak light from the window at the far back of the corridor. Day was dawning.

"All clear," whispered Doug, close to her now.

Hair rose on Agnes's forearms. Jeez, the man trod softly. Could creep one out.

"Right," she mumbled and made for the grayish opening in haste.

Neither looking right nor left, she crossed to her own door in two giant strides and whirled around. Only when she sensed the reassuring strength of the solid door in her back did she release her breath in a soft whoosh.

Her fingers hadn't left the flashlight's spongy 'on' button and pressed it now of their own accord.

The door to Carmen's room stood firmly closed. Inside, she imagined Doug inspected every item from the bag at leisure.

Chapter 21

Only when she rounded the switchback of the staircase did Agnes slow down. The oil lamp's mellow light seemed bright coming out of the dimness. She pocketed her flashlight and exhaled slowly to calm herself. Nothing should betray they were on the killer's trail.

Sauntering down the last steps, she had a clear view of the sofa. Carmen appeared asleep in a fetal position, swaddled in a blanket pulled up to the chin. The woman's large frame wouldn't fit stretched out.

Theresa was no longer in the kitchen. Had she retired again to her own quarters? Something appeared different about the open space. It took a moment for Agnes to realize the curtains were open. Despite the gooey mess clinging to the panes, a green-tinged luminescence filtered through.

Agnes stared, transfixed, as though the evidence of daylight might prove an illusion like a fata morgana if she took another step.

Sonorous snoring issued from the sofa.

A strange, high-pitched echo whistled from the grandfather chair, startling Agnes. Moving closer, she saw their hostess's head cradled against the chair's padded wing. On Theresa's lap rested the woolen concoction she'd worked on in the afternoon. The long needles stood on guard, stabbed into the soft knitting.

Another whistling snore escaped when Agnes tiptoed by. Doug was right, Agnes thought. It would be cruel to inflict tidings of evil doings on the unwary proprietress.

Soft chuckling diverted Agnes's attention to the far corner of the living room. Rob beckoned to join him and his cousin at the occasional table the guys had used earlier.

"Good nap?" asked Rob, his voice low.

Kieran rose and grabbed another chair. For a hunky guy, he moved softly.

His gaze lingered on her face. "You don't look rested," he observed.

"Er. Couldn't sleep," she improvised, unwilling to lie outright. Still, a blush crept up her throat.

From the sofa came an explosive snorting, making Rob chortle. "Seems some don't have that problem," he whispered when a vibrating snuffle from the wing chair answered like the antistrophe of an ancient tragedy chorus.

Agnes stole an apprehensive glance over her shoulder at the sofa. Let sleeping killers lie. If Carmen slumbered until the police arrived, things would be much easier.

Sensing Kieran's questioning gaze, she whispered, "Will it be light enough soon to go for help? You think you can find this Joe? The farmer, I mean?"

Both cousins regarded her, Rob with raised brows and Kieran frowning.

"Reckon finding the farm's no trouble," Kieran said. "Another 10, 15 minutes, and I'll give it a shot."

His words triggered Agnes's anxiety about the gun. What if the sleeping killer had another weapon tucked away under the blanket? If he ventured out in quest of Farmer Joe, only Doug, the unsuspecting Rob, and she were left to deal with an awakening killer. Wouldn't it be best, after all, to loop in these guys?

She was about to speak when Rob's glance veered toward the stairs. Agnes twisted in her chair.

At the far end of the harvest table stood Douglas Junior, rubbing his hands. From the opposite corner of the spacious room, she couldn't detect any telltale bulge in his cardigan. He must have stored the gun. Now Agnes wondered if the deadly thing was safer on or off his person.

Doug toddled over. His expression somewhat inane, he peered at them.

Rob pointed at the sofa and the grandfather chair, and psst-ting, put his finger to his lips.

"Kieran's heading out shortly to get help," Agnes whispered to Doug. With a meaningful nod at the sofa, she added, "Contact police, we hope."

Doug arched a brow and turned to Kieran. Incredulity swung in his voice when he asked, "Alone?"

Like the cousins, Agnes frowned.

"Is that wise?" Doug insisted.

"Whyever not? What the heck are you getting at?" Kieran's voice rose a notch.

"Shhh." Discreetly, Rob pointed at the sleepers.

Agnes cast a glance at Carmen. Contrary to popular belief, evil had a soporific effect. No conscience appeared to ruffle the criminal mind.

Instead of answering, Doug went to grab a chair. The way he placed it seemed strategic to Agnes. Keep everyone in view yet close enough for a quiet conversation.

Hands folded in his lap, he ogled them through his spectacles as if shortsighted. If Agnes hadn't already noticed the lenses were like window glass, she might have fallen for the act.

"I'm sure you gentleman know best," he said ponderously, then peered at Rob as if responsibility rested with the younger cousin. "I'm wondering, is it quite safe for Kieran here to sally forth without the means of calling for backup?"

Makes it sound like an arctic mission, Agnes thought.

"Eh?" Rob wrinkled his nose.

Doug raised both forefingers. "If the magnificent trees around this house can snap like matchsticks." He twisted his hands as if breaking a stick in the air. "What tremendous destruction will lie in wait out there?" His head swayed from side to side.

Taken aback at having missed this obvious danger, Agnes's eyes widened.

"Like as not, be some awful." Kieran seemed unperturbed.

"Didn't you mention last evening trees leaning over the drive, ready to smash the unwary?" Doug asked. "The hurricane must have uprooted many more during the night. A truly dangerous situation."

The image of the giant spruce felled at the backdoor flashed in Agnes's mind. Horrific contemplating anyone being in its path when it crashed down. A hefty branch could kill a man. The wind probably remained potent for a while.

Rob nodded. "You've got a point, sir. On the job, it's the rule not to go it alone. And that's with phones working."

"A sound policy. That's settled, then." Doug nodded as if they all agreed. "One of you can accompany this farmer to the police, and the other report back here." His raised arm forestalled objections. "Provided it is safe for one man to return alone."

He turned to Agnes as if taking her concurrence for granted. "We won't mind waiting."

Non-committal, she mumbled, "If you think so."

"I do," he said firmly.

His eyes on the box that held the pieces of the chess game he'd lost earlier, Kieran flapped the container's tiny clasp with roughened fingers.

"Got it all worked out, have you, mate?" His tone was mildly offensive. Nothing like his cousin's well-mannered politeness. "'Tis all the same to me," he added and pushed away the wooden box.

With a slight head movement, he caught Rob's attention and jutted his chin toward the rear opposite side of the room. "Let's get'er done."

"Stay safe, you two," murmured Agnes and reached out to skinny Rob just shy of touching him. Somehow, their departure felt like abandonment.

"Hey, no worries, Agnes. We'll be back in no time with the cavalry." His ever-ready smile sought to reassure her as he offered a high-five in jest.

Kieran eyed her closely. "You OK? Not headachy or something?"

"I'm fine," she insisted, more to convince herself. "Just worried about you guys going out there."

"Don't. Danger comes with the job." Kieran grinned at his cousin but spoke to Agnes. "You should see that little monkey swing high up in a huge sucker of a maple. Gotta be agile cutting down or tethering trees."

A soft, chimp-like pant hoot from Rob startled Agnes. His grin was infectious. Of course, she thought, as a firefighter, Kieran dealt with tons of dicey situations that put his life on the line. How did he deal with all that stress when his full-time job was as hazardous as his volunteering? Quite the guy. And Rob was no slouch either.

"C'mon, monkey." Kieran slapped his cousin's shoulder. "Time's a wastin'."

Doug, who'd sat contemplating his fingernails as if wondering about a manicure, said in the feeble voice Agnes saw as his camouflage, "Good luck, gentlemen. We shall await your safe return."

The cousins circumnavigated the sofa and aimed for the front foyer.

Agnes frowned. Did they intend to clamber down the collapsed porch? Then she realized their outdoor gear must still be there.

Uncomfortable in this corner with Doug for company, she followed the cousins as they crossed the kitchen, boots in hand. They aimed for the hopefully still unobstructed side entrance by the pantry.

Silently, she stood by while they laced their work boots and donned rain jackets that looked damp.

"Here goes," Kieran said, his hand on the doorknob.

When he opened the door, gray daylight poured in. Agnes heard the wind's rush nowhere near the roar of the night, yet powerful enough to drive the rain at a sharp angle.

"You'll get soaked again," she said as if that were the only concern.

"No big deal," Rob said. "Don't worry about a thing." He pulled up his hood and yanked at its cord. With the cord stopper locked, the hood crunched up around his face, leaving just his eyes and nose exposed.

"Cheerio," he mumbled through the fabric covering his lips. The skin around the eyes crinkled in a grin.

"Keep safe," she repeated her injunction.

"Will do." Kieran's sober gaze lingered. "Don't let that man spook you, Agnes."

She nodded and watched until, rounding the corner of the house, they were out of sight. The rain spat into her face as she leaned forward. This side of the house must be protected from the storm's force. Yet she could see branches and brush tossed helter-skelter. Green-brown confetti from fragmented vegetation littered the ground. Among them, she detected pieces of asphalt shingles from the roof. Several trees leaned crookedly onto their neighbors in a drunk embrace.

What she first assumed to be a mound of dirt and debris where the guys cornered the house toward the drive, she now recognized as a giant root ball of a fallen tree. Doug was right. Venturing out after a hurricane was truly hazardous.

Reluctantly, she closed the door and wiped raindrops off her face. Even her hair felt damp when she stroked back the strands that clung to her cheeks. Still, the raw air refreshed after an indoor atmosphere stale from spent emotions.

When she returned to the kitchen, she found Doug enthroned at the stair end of the harvest table. The room lay in murky dimness, illuminated only by the greenish light from the windows and three or four tea lights. Doug must have extinguished the oil lamp. Or it burned out.

After a whiff of fresh air, the inside felt stifling. With a start, Agnes noticed another difference. When had the snoring ceased?

She side-stepped the sofa for a peek at the sleeper. Carmen had rolled over and now faced the backrest. The blanket pulled up to the crown of her short-shorn head shrouded the woman's face.

In the stillness, Agnes heard rhythmical breathing. A glance at the grandfather chair confirmed Theresa rested quietly, too. Was snoring contagious? If one stopped, so did the other? A tiny grin at the idea curved Agnes's lip.

Worry set in again. How long before the sleepers awoke? Once Theresa was up and prattled noisily in the kitchen, Carmen was bound to wake, too. Then, preventing her escape would rest on Doug and Agnes.

How stop a killer determined to flee? Or should they let her go and count on the cops to catch her en route to the mainland?

Chapter 22

An awkward twosome with Doug at the table didn't appeal to Agnes. She wanted to listen to the news. Not an option right now. The ancient radio's infernal crackling would wake the dead. Never mind the sleepers.

Dealing with an escaping killer on an empty stomach after a sleepless night was more than she could stomach. Avoid noise and hope for police riding to the rescue.

Of different opinion, her innards issued a gurgling growl. Embarrassed, Agnes glanced at the man. Wrong move. He beckoned to join him.

She padded around his chair and grabbed a seat on the kitchen side. This way, she could keep an eye on the sofa's back in case the killer rose.

"Hungry?" Doug's mouth twitched.

"I'd give a lot for hot coffee," Agnes admitted. "No chance of that."

"My poison is bacon and eggs." The man grinned like they were conspirators. Well, maybe they were.

"Scrambled eggs with salmon. Plus, croissants hot from the oven." Agnes's mouth salivated but from mild nausea at the mental image. It brought back disconcerting memories. The fare a friend in Germany had dished up after a gruesome encounter with death.

"You love your cholesterol, too, I see." His toothy smile revealed pointed canines she hadn't noticed before. Then again, chatty bonhomie was a new development.

Restlessness made her itchy. Should she leave Doug on guard and dash to her room? Splash some water from the jug on her face and freshen up?

Grubbiness after a long, sleepless night left her at a disadvantage. She needed her wits on high alert when the police arrived.

She inched her chair back and rose. The man watched her with a questioningly raised brow.

"I'll be right back," she whispered. "You'll keep watch, won't you?"

"Most certainly. Take your time." His pink hands rubbed in a circular washing motion.

Something deeply psychological about that, Agnes figured.

"You got your…" she crooked her forefinger like pulling a trigger.

"Of course." With a disconcerting, slow wink, he patted his midriff.

Her brows shot up, thinking, hope the safety catch is on. He'd regret it if the thing went off in an awkward spot.

Softly, she made for the stairs and tiptoed up to minimize the treads creaking. From the halfway landing, she glanced back. Neither Carmen nor Doug had stirred, as far as she could tell from this angle. Of Theresa, she saw nothing behind the chair's bulky back.

Glad of a few minutes' respite, Agnes mounted the stairs to the lobby. On an impulse, she crossed over to the window and pulled the heavy curtains.

No luck. The panes were so thickly coated, only the merest glimmer of daylight filtered through. Her hands went to the levers, tempted to slide up the sash. They dropped of their own accord. Better not risk the sodden leafy mess blowing in. Mopping floors was not an option now. Assessment of the storm's devastation must wait.

Agnes hurried along the corridor that struck her as less dim than an hour ago. Its nighttime pitch darkness seemed a faint memory already.

As she opened her door, she wondered how the guys were making out. Their groundskeeper jobs equipped them best for dealing with the post-hurricane conditions out there. Tough and resourceful types.

So was Carmen, her mind added. A barbell-swinging girl, the woman had called herself. If she escaped, she'd manage alright. Only needed to make it down the drive to the highway to hitch a ride. Would traffic resume already?

The stuffiness inside her room hit Agnes full force. Airing out must wait until she had time for the inevitable clean-up of the goo.

Instead, she aimed for the bathroom and performed minimal ablutions. A cat would do a better grooming job, she figured wryly as she applied facial cleanser with a cotton pad. Barely 24 hours since taking a shower, and her skin thirsted for another. She certainly wouldn't indulge in a bubble bath for a long time. Bound to trigger memories of floating bodies.

Back in the bedroom, she slipped on clean jeans, a long-sleeved T-shirt, and a zip-up fleece for warmth. As she transferred her wallet and phone from the heap of discarded clothes into her jacket, she was tempted to linger.

No, she must see this through to the bitter end. With renewed purpose, she straightened her spine and made for the door.

About to reach for the knob, the door burst open before her hand touched it. Agnes jumped back in reflex.

Killer Carmen stood framed against the grayish light of the hall-way, almost filling the opening. She, too, had changed pants but still wore the navy sweatshirt that hung loosely over the black jeans.

"What are you staring at me for?" Carmen grunted. "You said I could use your can."

"Er, um. Sure. No problem," mumbled Agnes. Then anger propelled her assertiveness and displaced rising fear. "You startled me, bursting in like that. Could have knocked me right over."

Wrong phrase to use, Agnes realized, as Carmen's eyes narrowed. Did the woman know they were on to her?

"Are ya gonna let me in, or what?" The wide-legged stance reinforced the snarl.

"Be my guest." In stepping sideways, the back of Agnes's legs knocked against the edge of the bed. Her hand groped for the headboard post to steady herself.

Carmen smirked and strode past, straight to the bathroom. From there, she glanced over her shoulder, saying with exaggerated sarcasm, "Don't bother waiting for me. I see myself out."

When the door closed behind the woman's massive back, Agnes's glance darted over the room. No way she'd hang around waiting. If Carmen was into small-time pilfering, besides robbing stores and shooting people, so be it. Few things of value here.

Agnes patted her pockets for the phone and wallet and hurried to the door. Time to warn Doug of Carmen's imminent departure.

Minutes later, Agnes hesitated on the halfway stair landing. Doug's chair set empty. She took the last steps at a double, her eyes searching the open space. No sign of the man.

Maybe he followed Carmen up and held watch in his room, Agnes surmised. She'd hastened along the corridor, not looking right or left. If his door were a crack open, she wouldn't have noticed.

As she stood still, a soft, whistling snore punctuated the stillness. It wasn't even silence. Like an ill-tuned radio at threshold volume, the wind's droning permeated the stale air.

Agnes padded over to the kitchen counter and grabbed a bottle from a 24-pack by the broom closet. She twisted the cap and downed half the water in one go. Her stomach gurgled in response.

Footsteps thumped on the wooden stair treads.

Warily eying the staircase, Agnes took another swig. For a split second, she regretted not having armed herself with a butcher's knife from the block on the counter. Only to reject the idea as insane. If anything, it would put her in danger of having it turned against herself. With zero experience in armed combat, she'd have no chance against a 200-pound-plus woman, even if no gun was involved.

Dressed as before, Carmen strode along the harvest table and ignored Agnes, backed against the counter.

As the woman passed her, Agnes saw a soft-shell pack dangling from one shoulder. Its thin nylon bulged as if crammed full.

Agnes's mind raced in tandem with her heart. Should she challenge Carmen? Better wait. Where was Doug when needed?

She watched Carmen strut to the foyer and return booted and clad in black rain gear. A black beanie pulled down over the eyebrows hid the short-shorn hair.

No way you could tell male or female, Agnes thought. The woman could easily fake a masculine swagger. Pass for a man any day. Shroud the face behind a full-mask balaclava for a perfect disguise.

If stopped by police, the Valkyrie only needed to ramp up feminine charm, add a hip-swinging gait, or girlish chatter to disarm them.

Now, Carmen made straight for the counter, causing Agnes to stiffen.

"What?" The woman's sneer from above dwarfed Agnes. "Surprised I'm leaving?"

"Um. No. Not really." Agnes cleared her throat and added firmly, "You said you would."

Agnes's eyes strayed to the stairs. Still no Doug. Did he revert to his useless persona during this moment of crisis? How was she to prevent the killer's escape armed with an empty plastic bottle?

"Do you mind?" Carmen hissed. Her bulk towered closer.

Instinctively, Agnes ducked sideways and promptly felt foolish when Carmen grabbed two bottles from the pack on the counter, stuffing them into the pockets of the voluminous rain jacket.

"Say hi to the cops for me, " she scoffed and hooted like it was a hilarious joke.

Still laughing raucously, her boots clattered over the plank floor to the side exit by the pantry. The door banged like a shot.

A delayed tremor had Agnes lean back against the counter. Her gaze panned to the stairs and on toward the back of the grandfather chair. Surely, anyone in the house, except for the dead, must've heard Carmen.

With a heartfelt sigh at her failure to prevent the killer's escape,

Agnes ambled around the table separating kitchen and living room. Pointless to avoid noise after the racket Carmen had made.

On moving closer to the capacious armchair, she saw Theresa's face peer around the chair's elephantine ears. The graying curls were tousled from sleep, and the upholstery fabric's pattern was imprinted on the reddened cheek. Yet Theresa's expression seemed alert.

How long had their hostess been awake?

"Sorry, Carmen was a bit noisy," Agnes said, attempting to seem normal.

Theresa's face pinched in a scowl. "Good riddance," she muttered. "Couldn't abide that hussy. Real rude, she was."

No more 'Carmen, dear,' Agnes noted. Theresa might well prefer Carmen out of the way when the police arrived. Chances were, Leo told Carmen about Theresa's past. She'd use that nice tidbit to divert the police's attention from herself.

"Well, there's that," Agnes commented.

Of course, thought Agnes, it would take seconds for the police to find out about Theresa. Their database would spit out the entire food poisoning case history in split seconds. Who knew what other info they recorded about people's past?

Like yours, a renegade voice in her head insinuated. Done nothing criminal, reason objected. Sure, her name cropped up several times in connection with sudden death. Through no fault of her own—

A polite 'Ahem' from the stairs made her swivel around and do a double take.

It was Douglas Junior, but what a change. Clad in a dark blue tracksuit, a white stripe running along the sleeves and legs, he looked like a different man. His feet stuck in high trainers. Not a single hair protruded from the color-matched wooly hat. Most disturbing was the slight squint that made his eyes downright beady. He'd discarded the spectacles.

Annoyed at his tardy arrival, Agnes strode over and hissed softly, only for him to hear, "Where were you? She's done a bunk. I thought you'd stop her."

Like a comedy conspirator, he put a finger to his lips and jutted his chin toward the grandfather chair.

Their hostess's head poked around the chair's wing. Reaching up one hand to pat the tufted hair flat, she cried, "Why, there's Dougie. Going for a jog?" As if that were the most natural thing in the wake of a hurricane.

"Not quite, dear Mrs. Mae." Doug sashayed over and stood by the chair. "Taking stock of the damage, you might say. My car is my livelihood. I cannot afford to lose her."

"Right, you are." Theresa nodded and wriggled her rear end to the edge of the wide seat. While Theresa's swollen feet angled for her furry slippers, Doug pivoted on his heels.

With a slow wink at Agnes, he hurried to the side door in his mincing gait. There, he shook a thin waterproof from a pouch around his waist and pulled it over his head.

Agnes wanted to shout 'Wait up,' but it might raise Theresa's curiosity.

Prepared for the elements, Doug saluted with a pink palm to his temple.

"So long, dear ladies," he called cheerily and left Agnes standing, mouth agape.

Chapter 23

Agnes stood transfixed. Did Doug care only about the safety of his car? Or was he going after Carmen? Why then leave it so late?

The woman had a head-start. Plus, far longer legs than Doug and could vault any obstructions in her path.

"Intrepid, I call the fellow." Theresa beamed.

It was the last adjective Agnes would have picked to describe the man. 'Useless' came to mind again.

"Young Kieran and Rob might take a leaf from his book." Theresa pointed to the ceiling. "Bet they're asleep like babes in arms up there."

"You'd lose your bet. They've gone out at first light in quest of Farmer Joe. While you had your little nap," Agnes added and immediately regretted the pettishness.

"Goodness. I didn't sleep. Just rested my eyes for a minute."

Agnes quelled the rejoinder that, awake, she couldn't have missed the cousins' exit. Instead, she said casually, "I think I'll venture out, too. Storm's abating. Fresh air will do me good."

"Mind you stay close," said her hostess and eyed her as if she suspected some ulterior design. Like stalking Doug. Which wasn't far from the truth, Agnes had to admit.

Aloud, she said, "I'll report back on the state of your yard."

That got Theresa's nodding approval. "Run along, then, dear. Mind checking the hen house? Tell my cluckers mother be out in a jiffy with brekky mash."

"Will do," Agnes called back, already halfway to the foyer to grab outerwear.

Boots in hand, she rushed to the side exit before Theresa could scramble to her stubby legs.

The wellies, still slightly damp, seemed even flabbier than last afternoon when they braved the storm. Definitely a couple of sizes too big. Wrapped in her jacket, she sallied forth.

Islanders would call the wind a fair breeze, she thought wryly, as a vicious gust whipped the hood off her head. She twisted her hair into a loose coil at the nape and fastened the hood's drawstrings. Tightened, it impeded vision, she found when she glanced in both directions to determine which way to go.

Hands dug deep into the jacket pockets, she rushed along the house wall in the direction she'd seen the cousins take. The hens would have to wait for their mistress's message.

Rubber boots squelching through sodden leaves, she tripped several times over branches and piles of slippery twigs. Rain beat against her cheeks, making her blink.

When she rounded the corner, a mountain of greenery blocked her path. The toppled spruce at the backdoor splayed its massive branches like wings. Its spiky limbs reached far into the dense shrubbery on the other side of the path and entangled with evergreen kith and kin.

Should she go back and try the opposite side, past the chicken coop? She promised to check on the creatures. Not a priority now. The cousins struck out this way and succeeded. Else she'd seen them return while she lingered at the door.

Mind made up, Agnes moved along the periphery of the spruce's carcass. Its branches whipped back and forth with every gust as if determined to lash her. Close up, the shrubbery showed a gap where others must have plowed through. Though the broken twigs might be the storms doing, the deep footprints in the soggy soil of the border were not.

To shield her face, Agnes pushed through backwards with no idea what awaited behind. Though Theresa had mentioned plans for meandering walking trails on the expansive property, urbanite Agnes never explored the wood lot. Right now, it was a tangled mass of undergrowth, which the hurricane had spiked with hazardous forest debris. Above her, the trees' creaking and groaning boded ill.

Costs to clear this without bulldozing the whole lot, thus destroying its appeal, would be prohibitive, Agnes figured as she stared at the humongous root balls of an entire row of downed coniferous trees. Strangely, the hurricane felled the healthy ones. A few dead trees stretched their scrawny, naked crowns heavenward like accusing fingers.

Stop dawdling and find a way to the drive, her mind ordered as she clambered over a tree trunk.

The sloppy gumboots hampered her progress. Nor was she quite sure of the direction. Well aware of the drive snaking its way from the road for several hundred yards, she couldn't tell the shortest distance to it. Nothing for it but plowing on.

Drenched by rain and dripping brushwork, Agnes felt water-logged inside her boots. Branches had pulled down her hood, and twigs ensnared her wet hair. When she broke backwards through yet another coniferous wall, she sensed gravel underfoot. The drive.

Where she stood, the drive curved. Agnes's fingers forked sodden strands of hair from her face. She glanced in both directions. A tree leaned precariously on her left. The house must be somewhere to her right, she surmised.

With quite a head start, Carmen must long have passed this point. So must Doug.

On the open drive, the wind hit her full force. Agnes stuffed her tresses back under the hood and strode left. Past the curve, the drive dipped. Now she knew where she was. It descended to the hollow, where it crossed the brook. The one with the leaning hemlock that Kieran had pronounced a goner.

She'd noticed the majestic evergreen many times in passing. What a shame if the venerable giant fell victim to the storm.

Several slimmer trees obstructed her path as she hastened on. Deep furrows carved by the deluge caused her to stumble. Agnes no longer could tell if her skin was wet from rain or sweat.

As she rounded a curve near the bottom of the decline, Kieran's prediction proved correct. The ancient tree lay sprawled across the drive. Maneuvering the barricade meant crossing the swollen brook. Her feet, squelching in the wellies, could hardly get much wetter.

Or so she thought until her boots sank ankle-deep into muddy water before even reaching the brook's bed. Which way to round the fallen giant? Root-ward or crown-ward?

How the heck did the others get through?

Root-ward, she went, eyes scanning the ground for tripping hazards. Agnes groped her way along the hemlock's boughs that blocked her vision. When alive and well, the tree appeared 100 feet tall. On its back, it still looked gigantic.

The closer she got to its roots, the deeper her oversized boots sank into mud, covered by murky water that sloshed over their rim. Every step required an effort to dislodge them.

Frustrated, Agnes stopped, ready to give up and beat a retreat. She scanned her position to see if returning was easier than going forward.

Ahead of her, the hemlock stretched its soil-encased feet skyward. Another few yards and she might peek around the upturned roots. Though other trees crowded both sides of what now was a stream, the water might be clear enough beyond the vast hole caused by the fallen tree. It would allow her to see obstacles before fording the waters.

Into the swooshing of the wind burst a ferocious cry. A mix of anger and fear, it sounded like.

Agnes dragged her feet from the mud's greedy embrace and stumbled forward. A rank stench emanated from the boggy crater gouged by the felled tree.

Once she could see beyond the hemlock's sprawling roots, she spotted Carmen on her belly in the stream, propped up precariously on her forearms.

On Agnes' side, across from Carmen, stood Doug. His feet immersed in water, he pointed a gun at the woman.

They hadn't noticed her, half concealed by the hemlock's root ball. Or paid no heed. With bated breath, Agnes assessed the situation. Doug seemed in control. Better not distract him.

A vicious wind gust distorted beyond recognition whatever Doug called to Carmen. Agnes assumed he ordered her to come out of the water.

Carmen's torso rose on her extended arms like a cobra. Even from a distance, the woman's broad features appeared contorted in rage or fright.

"Then shoot me," Carmen cried.

Stunned, Agnes watched Doug point the gun straight at Carmen's chest.

"I will." His voice came loud and clear.

What in hell was going on? Shielded by the tree roots, Agnes inched forward, readying to step in.

Doug's laugh shocked her more than the menacing tone. "You'll find drowning preferable to bleeding to death."

Carmen howled like a cornered animal.

"I'll speed it up," he shouted. "Push you under."

A closet sadist, Agnes's mind shrieked. Revels in making the Valkyrie grovel. A power game.

Feverishly, her brain untangled, impressions flashing back. In an epiphany, she saw why Leo had to die.

"No!" Carmen's anguished outcry burst into Agnes's momentary distraction. The cry dissolved into sobs.

Please, no, Agnes wanted to shout. Don't break down. Worst reaction to a guy's power trip.

Might he prolong his pleasure of having a weakened prey at his mercy? Agnes's mind raced. Buy time. No way to go for help. Act before he tires of the game. Save Carmen's life.

Another part of her mind reeled at risking her own safety in protecting a criminal who most likely was a killer. Only to be vetoed by her moral monitor's promptings. A human is a human. Innocent until proven guilty. Don't stray from the rule of law.

Agnes swallowed hard and cleared her throat. Afraid of startling Doug and forcing his hand, she 'ahem—ed' a few times softly and emerged from the shelter. He didn't react.

With a step out into the open, she called, "Good for you, Doug. You caught her."

Doug whirled around. The gun's muzzle swung from Carmen to Agnes, causing her heart to miss a beat and accelerate.

Saliva pooled in her mouth as Doug's eyes darted to Carmen and back.

Talk him down, reason urged. Like they do with hostage-takers and potential suicides.

Frozen in the moment and rooted to the spot, a sinking sensation pervaded her. The ground literally sucked down her boot deeper and deeper.

Say something! her frantic mind prodded.

She gulped for breath and called, "Let's get her out of the water. She won't run off."

Loud splashing alerted Agnes. Doug pivoted at the sound. The gun swayed back to Carmen, whose arms flayed wildly, hitting the water as she scrambled for a foothold. Now, she managed a shaky crouch.

If the woman really had another gun, it would be soaked by now in the icy water, flashed through Agnes's mind.

"Don't move!" Doug shouted. Muzzle pointed at Carmen, he yelled, "Okay, Agnes, it's safe now. Come over and help."

"Don't!" Carmen's yelp echoed a voice in Agnes's head. "He's gonna kill us."

Doug laughed. "Don't be a silly ass."

A sudden movement from behind startled Agnes. Before she could react, an arm slung around her waist and yanked her backwards in one powerful move. Her feet slipped out of the mud-locked boots, socks dragging through frigid water.

Her body collided with her rescuer's.

"Get back behind me." Kieran's head loomed over hers.

One-handed, he swung her around into the shelter of the hemlock.

"Stay put," he said.

As he stepped forward, she saw his right arm cock a rifle.

Where did that come from? Canadians don't bear arms. Unless they go hunting. The irony of her mental ricochet distracted Agnes for a second. Plenty of firearms around here.

"Drop that gun and stick'em up," Kieran yelled, aiming at Doug.

A second later, Kieran hollered, "Don't even think of it. This sucker's gonna blow your legs to pieces. Nasty things, hunting rifles."

Though Agnes no longer could see Doug with Kieran's hulk blocking her vision, she figured the man aimed at Kieran.

Kieran's calm "That's better" indicated Doug obeyed and dropped the gun.

Taking this for an 'all clear,' Agnes crept from the shield of upended roots that had towered even over Kieran's six-foot-something.

Ahead, Doug stood empty-handed, his arms raised high. Her stockinged feet immersed in murky water, Agnes waded a pace. Just in time to see Carmen bounce up, whirl around and splash to the opposite side of the stream.

"She's getting away." Agnes cried in frustration.

"No, she won't." Rob's shout carried over from across the water.

In a mix of fear for his safety and admiration for his daring, she watched him emerge from among the trees on that side.

A burly figure in a yellow sou'wester joined Rob. Like Kieran, the bearded guy held a rifle, its snout pointed at the ground. Though she had no recollection of the man, Agnes surmised it was Joe, the farming neighbor.

Shoulders sagging, a dripping Carmen slouched toward the pair as if resigned to her fate. The involuntary cold bath must have knocked the fighting spirit out of her.

"We'll bring her back the other way," Rob shouted. "Meet you at the house."

"For sure." Kieran raised his free hand in salute. "C'mon, man. Get a move on," he told Doug.

To Agnes, he said quietly, "Stay off to the side. Soon him and me pass, go pick up that gun. Be mighty careful. It'll be loaded."

"Will do," she said with some trepidation.

"Keep your distance on the way back. Don't want complications."

Her eyes on Doug, she watched him slosh through the muddy water, sure to have ruined his white trainers. She moved well out of reach should he plan a sudden lunge to use her as a human shield. His scowl sought to intimidate.

Only when Kieran had the man safely in front of him and herded him along the hemlock's trunk to the drive did she venture to the spot where Doug had stood.

After several minutes of cautious fishing in the brownish-green brew, she struck lucky. Her fingertips sensed an unyielding rounded cylinder. The gun's muzzle. With bated breath, she let them slide along to find the gun's butt and gingerly lifted it out of the water.

Impossible for her to tell if the slimy thing was the one they'd seen in Carmen's room. The size seemed about right. Guns were foreign objects to Agnes.

Forensics could tell if this one killed the cashier, she thought. So, of course, could the killer.

Just in case the water hadn't destroyed all prints, she dug for some tissues in her jacket pocket to hold the gun by.

The offending object held at arm's length, she splashed back to retrieve the useless wellies and headed for the house.

One thing beat her, she mused. Why did Kieran and Farmer Joe return bearing arms?

Chapter 24

By the time she reached the house, Agnes was panting for breath and thoroughly miserable. The gun in her hand frightened her more than the treacherous trip through boggy water and the woods. Pouring the slimy water from the wellies made little difference to soaked wool socks.

On the backside of the house, she paused. Take the gun inside? Not a good idea, she decided. Safer to conceal it out of Doug and Carmen's reach in case they broke loose. The hens wouldn't mind keeping their beady eyes on the gun until the police arrived.

Firearm wrapped in a rag and securely stored in a chicken feed bin, Agnes breathed deeply before opening the B&B's side entrance.

Had the guys remembered to tell the police this was the only unobstructed entry? No matter. The cops were savvy enough to figure that out.

As soon as she opened the door, she heard voices raised in anger. A wave of utter exhaustion made her lean against the jamb. She kicked off the wellies, her ears straining to catch what was going on. Stripping off socks and rain jacket, she thought of how frantic Theresa must be, confronted with her guests returned at gunpoint.

It propelled her forward through the passage, barefooted and soggy jeans clinging to her legs.

Now, she could make out Doug's voice that rose over the others.

"Assault with a weapon," he yelled. "Forced confinement. My lawyers will sue the pants off you!"

The irony of the man's accusation boosted Agnes' spirits.

"You're a hoot." Carmen's comment sounded hoarse and flat.

Past the pantry, where the passage opened into the living space, Agnes almost bumped into Joe. He propped up the wall, rifle in the crook of his arm.

Dangerous loitering in the pathway, flitted through her mind. Made sense, though, to block the only escape route, short of climbing through a window.

The farmer's massive bulk impeded her view. With a tiny cough, she sought his attention in the hope not to startle him. "Er... excuse me."

He didn't even twitch. Just hollered, "Lady to see you, Mrs. M."

Down by the brook he probably didn't notice her, hidden behind the hemlock carcass.

"That'll be Agnes," Theresa called.

Their hostess would be in the kitchen, the comfort zone in any crisis. Clattering of dishes confirmed Agnes's assumption.

Joe moved aside, unhurried.

Upon entering, Agnes's eyes swept the open-concept living area and immediately saw Doug and Carmen in straight-backed chairs, two yards apart, smack in the middle of the room. Their chairs faced the kitchen side, their backs to the living room windows.

Carmen, swaddled in blankets from head to toes, spotted her first and hissed in Doug's direction, "She saw you." Then hollered at Agnes, "You heard him yell he'd shoot me."

"Hang on," came Rob's voice from the wings. "Don't lead your witness."

Agnes hadn't immediately seen him with the voluminous grandfather chair in the way. He hovered near the 'Private' door.

"He's right, you know," Kieran commented from the other side by the front entrance foyer. His rifle, also tucked underarm, pointed to the floor.

"Whatever." Carmen's favorite rejoinder lacked its dismissive force.

Agnes tried to ignore Doug's calculating stare. First, she'd thought he'd crossed his arms behind the chair, as some people do. His straining posture when he sought her attention told her his hands were tied.

Head held high, he said to Kieran, "You will find Dr. Taylor can vouch for me." Turning pointedly to Agnes, he urged, "Tell them what we discovered." Voice lowered and insinuating, "Your word will carry more weight with these people."

While he spoke, Theresa bustled over from the kitchen, a scoop and a jar in hand. Oblivious to the volatile tension, her attention focused solely on Agnes's legs, mouth opening in a wide O.

"Goodness," she cried. "Look at your pants. Wet like a drowned rat, you are. Dear me." With a volley of tut-tutting, she wagged a finger at Kieran but told Agnes, "I said to them, it's one thing for a man to get a soaking. Us women are different. We catch cold real quick."

"It's okay, Theresa," Agnes assured her, amazed this was the older woman's only reaction to prisoners at gunpoint in her living room. "Oh, and your hens are fine. I delivered your message."

Theresa shook the jar. "Brekkie's almost ready. Just need to add their vitamins." Using the scoop as a scolding finger, she pointed at Agnes's jeans. "Go put on dry clothes, dear."

"What about me?" Carmen cried from across the room. "I'm a lot wetter than her." The last bit came quietly, without rancor.

"I'll get you some dry stuff," Agnes said. "You can change in the downstairs loo." She turned to Kieran. "Can't she?"

He shrugged. "Guess so."

"Agnes! Enough is enough." Doug's outburst forced Agnes to acknowledge him. She'd studiously avoided Doug's scowling face while aware of him straining against whatever confined his arms behind his back.

"I suggest we end this farce," he said acidly. "My patience has its limits. Tell them what really happened. Or—"

"Oh, I will." Agnes kept her face bland. "Hang in there." She turned to their hostess, who'd grown restive. "Do you mind a quick word, Theresa? In your room, if that's okay."

Not only Doug frowned at that. Kieran, too, shot her a questioning glance. Head tilting back, Carmen contemplated the ceiling. Agnes's quick glance at the farmer found him impassive, his jaws moving rhythmically like chewing over these odd going-ons. Only Rob seemed eager with anticipation.

Theresa looked unhappy. "Can't it wait? My cluckers need feeding."

"This is a madhouse," cried Doug.

Conscious of Kieran's puzzled gaze, Agnes told him, "Be right back."

"Got you," he said. "Mind, be quick. Reckon police be here any minute."

Agnes's fingers touched Theresa's elbow. "Okay? Won't take a few moments." With the gentlest pressure, she steered the reluctant lady toward the private entry.

When Theresa tried to stall and speak, Agnes muttered, "Later."

Once the door separating Theresa's domain from the living room was firmly closed behind them, Agnes said, "Is there a way to open the wardrobes? We need to check something upstairs."

"Why? Did you lose your key, dear? No big deal. I keep master keys in case folks take the keys along when they go home. You wouldn't believe the stuff some people take along. Or leave behind."

"Oh, I would," Agnes said, remembering the jumble in Theresa's medicine cabinet. "If you don't mind grabbing the master keys to the rooms and the wardrobes, let's go up. Er, and a pair of rubber gloves too, please."

"You don't need me for that, Agnes. I'll just give you the keys and go see to my hens."

"Not yet. I need you with me, please." Seeing a stubborn expression rise to Theresa's face, she added, "It's really important. For you too."

"If you say so, dear." The frown and headshake showed Theresa far from convinced.

Chapter 25

A few minutes later, they entered the upper hallway from the backstairs entry. When they drew level with Agnes's room and she didn't stop, Theresa said, "But dear, where are you taking me? Won't you go in and change?"

"No time now. First things first." With a grumbling Theresa in her wake, Agnes strode toward the opposite end of the ill-lit corridor and stopped in front of Doug's room.

"Unlock, please," she told her hostess. "We need to go in."

"In Dougie's room? Whatever for?" Theresa looked taken aback. Then her puckered brow uncreased. "Ah. You want to get him dry clothes. That's mighty nice of you."

"Er... It's more about... You'll see," Agnes muttered as Theresa unlocked.

Inside, she had to stop Theresa from marching straight to the wardrobe.

"Um, Theresa? This is actually about something else. There's a good reason the guys put Douglas Junior under restraints. And Carmen too. I want you to video me while I check something in his wardrobe. Just in case there's trouble later."

"Goodness, I heard the terrible things that hussy said about

175

Dougie. I'm sure he meant no harm. I grant you, Carmen is a wrong one."

Agnes slipped her hands into the rubber gloves. "I hate to disillusion you," she said gently. "He really threatened to shoot Carmen and meant it."

When only tongue-clicking answered her, Agnes glanced at her hostess. The older woman's relationship with Doug perplexed her more than ever. How had she reacted when Kieran brought the man back at gunpoint and presumably tied him to a chair? Would she defend Doug to the police?

Some sense of what to expect would help, Agnes decided and said, "Before I deep dive into Doug's stuff, just one question, Theresa. Are you very fond of the man?"

"Oh, dear me." Theresa's cheeks creased as she chuckled and shook a playful finger at Agnes. "You're a romantic girl, aren't you? Bet you thought me and Dougie were being naughty."

"Well... No, not with him having five kids. I mean, you call him Dougie. Makes it sound like you're on close terms."

Theresa's face puckered, transforming it from mirth to sadness. "No, it's not that. It's just he reminds me so of our Dougie. Right from the get-go on his first stay last year."

"Who's the other Dougie?" Agnes asked softly.

"Why, my dear brother. Didn't your mom tell you? Our Dougie was such a fine man. The head of the family from when Dad left us." Her hand reached to wipe her eyes. "Dougie passed away eight years ago. I still miss him sorely."

"I'm so sorry, Theresa. A terrible loss for you and your mother." Agnes felt bad about having reminded the older woman of her bereavement. Sera had never mentioned Theresa until the question of accommodation on PEI cropped up. But then again, Agnes reflected, she'd seen little of her own mom until this past year.

Theresa perked up, saying, "Douglas Junior is the spitting image of our Dougie. Could have knocked me down with a feather when he first stood at my door."

One mystery solved, Agnes figured, glad Theresa harbored no

passion for Doug. Things were complicated enough without deeper emotional strings.

"Okay, here goes," she said and pointed to the wardrobe. "Key, please."

Theresa fished an ordinary-looking key from her pocket and handed it over, reluctance written all over her puffy features. "Doesn't feel right snooping in my guests' rooms."

"Got to be done," Agnes said, firmer than she felt. "Tap record on my phone."

Theresa ambled sideways, aiming the phone's camera at Agnes.

"Er, no. Focus it on the cupboard and my hands, please. We want to video what we find in there."

"I'll try. Feels like in the movies."

With Theresa in the right position, Agnes unlocked the doors. A running commentary, she figured, might help if trouble with the cops arose later.

"I'm Agnes Taylor and am in Douglas Junior's room at Mrs. Mae's B&B," she muttered self-consciously.

"It's the Maple Lodge on Route 2," chirped her hostess. "It's me, Theresa Mae, behind the camera."

"Thanks, Theresa." With a glance to ensure the camera was focused on her hands, Agnes went on, "I'm about to open the wardrobe because I suspect Douglas Junior is concealing evidence of a crime. I'm acting as a precautionary measure to prevent him from disposing of anything incriminating before I can convince police to search his room."

Unless she could present conclusive evidence to the police before they even spoke to anyone else, the cops would misjudge the situation and focus on Kieran and Joe holding two people at gunpoint. If Doug threatened legal action, the cops might free him right away. They'd see no reason to search this room.

Her preemptive justification recorded, she swung open the doors. "Zoom in, please," she instructed.

The content proved a let-down. On one side of the split interior, several white and light-blue shirts hung on the rack, next to two gray suits, the pant legs dangling. A charcoal-colored coat hung in between, its hems partially covering a piece of luggage resting on the cupboard floor.

Two shelves on the left held a cardigan and a couple of striped PJs, neatly folded. On another shelf was a stack of towels and washcloths that Theresa provided. Presumably, socks and underwear would be in the dresser.

A lower shelf contained a gleaming pair of patent Oxfords with stretchers inserted. The middle shelf gave houseroom to a zippered toiletry bag.

"Zoom in for a closeup, please, while I open this," she instructed.

Nothing earth-shattering emerged. The usual male items, shaving kit, and aftershave, plus dental care products and deodorant, were all Agnes found.

She zipped up the bag and stood back, scrutinizing the cupboard.

"What are we looking for, dear?" Theresa sounded worried.

"Just give me a minute," Agnes said, distracted by her own thoughts. "Zoom in again."

Bending her knees, she crouched in front of the hanging rail side. Her hands parted the suits and coat to fully reveal the suitcase that stood upright closer to the doorframe than its size seemed to warrant.

She grabbed its sides with her gloved fingertips. Touching as little of the faux leather material as possible, she lifted it out. Its relatively low weight suggested the luggage was empty.

"Hm," she murmured. "Not sure the phone's flash gives enough light." Still crouching, she peered up at Theresa, hovering behind her shoulders. "Try to capture as much as you can of this."

"I've got a flashlight in my pocket. Small but mighty. Would that help, dear?"

"Perfect. Good thinking. Yes, please, shine the light right in here while you video." Agnes held the dangling pants to one side and scuttled out of the camera's line of vision.

"Why, it's only Dougie's dirty laundry," Theresa commented, bent low.

The flashlight picked out a black bag in the dark recesses of the wardrobe. White lettering read 'Wash Me,' underscored by a smiley.

With a sense of doing something underhanded, Agnes issued a belated caution. "Okay, Theresa, here's the crunch. What I'm about to do might get me into some trouble. Would you like to opt out for your own protection?" In a pinch, she ought to be able to manage videoing while diving into the bag. She'd much prefer a witness to the procedures.

"Goodness, I've seen Dougie's undies many a time," cried Theresa. When Agnes's brows shot up, she broke into merry guffawing. "Naughty girl. Not what I mean at all. I do his laundry when he stays for a few days. He pays, mind you."

"So, you're in? The cops might rap our knuckles for it." Never mind what the courts might do, Agnes added to herself.

"This is my house, Agnes. No one can stop me checking on the safety of my premises. If Dougie is a wrong one, as you all say, then I have the right to inspect my own cupboards."

No matter how flawed Theresa's logic might be, Agnes mused, her hostess should know the rights governing the hospitality industry, even if she was lax about its rules.

"Alright, here goes. Video what I'm doing." With a start, Agnes realized the camera probably hadn't stopped recording their every word.

So be it, she thought. Shows we discussed it.

She leaned in and, grabbing the bulging bag by its drawstrings, dragged it out of the wardrobe. About two feet tall, it was made of a rubberized material. Gingerly, she untied the knot and pulled the opening wide.

"Yuck!" Though she'd kind of expected it, the loathsome, sour stench hit her potently.

"Oh? What is it, dear?" Theresa asked, bending down, her head close to Agnes' shoulder.

"Don't you smell it?" Agnes asked, perplexed.

"Can't say I do. Sweaty dark cotton can be a bit smelly. Mind you, my nose hasn't been what it was for ages."

"Wow, if you can't smell this…" Agnes left it unfinished as realization dawned. If Theresa's loss of her olfactory capacity predated the Bracebridge incident, the fatal fish obtained from dubious sources could have stunk to high heaven without Theresa noticing anything amiss.

"Right," Agnes said and made a mental note to stick her nose into Theresa's fridge more often. A quest for iffy items may prolong life.

"I'll grab a clean towel and spread it on the floor before dumping out the contents of Douglas Junior's bag," she announced.

"Go ahead, dear. If Dougie's laundry is icky, it'll come out in the wash."

"Not likely you'll ever get to wash this load," Agnes murmured.

A moment later, she upended the bag slowly onto a white bath sheet. At first, a few dry items slipped out. With a light plonk, a sodden bundle followed.

Despite the disgusting stench, Agnes bent close and recognized the outer shell as a woolly garment. Doug's cardigan, its arms knotted tightly around whatever it contained.

"I'm going to untie this," Agnes announced for the video's sake.

The nauseating smell threatened to trigger her gagging reflex. She swallowed hard.

Unwrapped, a pair of dress pants, darkened by wetness and speckled with ominous tiny flecks, emerged. Tied into the pants was a shirt, which might have been white. Like a Russian doll effect, the shirt contained another bulky item that shined through in a dark hue.

In for a dime, Agnes figured, as she undid the knotted shirt sleeves.

"How ever did he get his clothes wet to the bone?" Theresa sounded genuinely puzzled. Then, her tone lightened. "Of course. He must have gone outside for a breath of air last night. That'll be his undies in there, I bet."

"You'd lose your money," Agnes said and focused on the smaller black bag she'd unwrapped from the shirt's stranglehold. A tough plastic material like those advertised for watersports, it seemed. "Get a good shot of it from all sides before I open it."

Once recorded in situ, Agnes opened its watertight closure. "Shine the light right inside, please."

As she'd come to expect, there was yet another bag inside of it. This one, however, of clear plastic. With pointed fingers, Agnes stripped the outer bag a little lower for a better shot of its content.

"Why, for Pete's sake!" cried Theresa. "What on earth does the man want with a sack of pills?"

"Sell them. Lucratively," Agnes said dryly. "This is fentanyl, I bet. The drug they warned about on the news."

"Why, I'd never!" Theresa almost dropped the phone. "In my house?" Her lips closed in a firm line. "That does it. I'm through with that man!"

Chapter 26

Minutes later, Agnes watched closely as Theresa locked Doug's door from the outside.

"I'll give that man a piece of my mind," Theresa said. "I'm that disappointed in him."

"Please, Theresa. Let me handle this until the police take over." Agnes dabbed Theresa's arm to prevent her from barging downstairs. "Not a word about what we discovered. Unless I say it," she added for honesty's sake.

"But dear. I can't have such going-ons in my house."

"Of course not. I know how you feel," Agnes soothed her. "Just bear with me. We want to make sure he can't weasel his way out."

"If you say so." The steam of righteousness evaporated as Theresa's mouth puckered. "Sera always says what a smart girl you are. She thinks the world of you."

This unexpected praise gave Agnes a fuzzy, warm glow. A much-needed boost to her flagging confidence in the wisdom of her actions.

"Trust me," she said firmly to convince them both and led the way to the central staircase.

When they reached the halfway landing, Agnes scanned the open space below. Nothing appeared to have changed during their 10- or

15-minute absence. Well, the captives were fixed in place, anyway. No sign of the police.

With Theresa in her wake, she went down the last steps.

Carmen spotted her first and boomed, "Did you bring my stuff?"

Shoot, thought Agnes, completely forgot.

Aloud, she said, "Sorry, not yet. Something cropped up. Didn't change either." She pointed to her jeans and only now noticed how foul they reeked. Her body heat had plastered them to her legs and released the bog odor.

"Goodness! Where's my head?" cried Theresa. "I'll run up now. Back in a jiffy."

"No!" Agnes instantly regretted the outburst and reduced the volume a notch. "Sorry, Theresa. We need you here. We all can change later. The police will come any minute."

Agnes ignored Carmen and Doug's protests and turned to Kieran. "Did the police say how long they'd be? Must be an hour by now."

Kieran pushed his shoulders from the wall, shrugging. His rifle leaned against the entryway's frame. Jutting his chin in the farmer's direction, he said, "Joe talked to them. Reckoned less explaining if a neighbor calls."

Agnes looked from Kieran to Joe, who'd drawn up a chair by the pantry corridor. "Um, I thought you drove to the detachment with your ATV."

The farmer raised a hand from the rifle resting across his knees and pointed at Rob, saying, "No need. Me and the young fella moseyed up to Skipp's place. Got one of them satellite phones, Skippy docs. Dairy farmer."

Cattle, presumably, needed quick attention in emergencies flashed through Agnes's mind.

When Joe leaned back without further explanation, she asked a little impatiently, "So, who talked to the cops?"

"That'll be me, lass," Joe said.

"Did they say when to expect them?"

"In due time. Got to give them credit. Plenty of accidents last night. Bound to be busy beavers today." The farmer nodded to his own words.

A tug at her sleeve drew Agnes's attention to Theresa, still standing at her elbow.

"Dear, my cluckers need feeding. Won't take a minute."

What if Theresa opened the chicken feed bin? Agnes fretted. How stupid to hide the gun in there. Too late to remedy now.

"Please, Theresa, hang on until police arrive. I tossed them a few handfuls of kernels." Her votive offering, Agnes admitted silently, wasn't compassionate but to stop the hens' racket at her intrusion into their coop.

Shoulders dropping and tut-tutting, their hostess ambled around the harvest table and sank into a chair on its kitchen side.

"Now, Agnes." Doug's voice. "I've been more than patient with this charade. Tell these jokers to untie me. My hands are numb."

"No! Don't," Carmen shouted. "He tried to kill me."

"I've no authority over anyone—"

Doug cut off Agnes's words. "Even these clods must see reason if you tell them what we found. I assume you double-checked for more evidence?"

How deluded can you get? Agnes blinked in disbelief. Did the man not see what was coming?

"How dare these men hold me at gunpoint," Doug blustered. "Unauthorized use of weapons. Illegal!"

"The rifles are perfectly legal, sir," said Rob, emphasizing the last word. "We've got a hunting license. Rifle's locked properly in the truck for rough jobs in New Brunswick. Gotta deal with bears and moose."

"Or vermin," said Joe from afar.

"That gives you no right to point a rifle at people," Doug countered.

The situation was getting out of hand, Agnes figured. She dragged out a chair to place it near the wall between the staircase and the private door. That way, she'd have everyone except the farmer in her line of vision.

To gain a modicum of the authority she could lay no claim to, she opted to stand behind her chair. Her hands on the high backrest, its wood infused a sense of solidity reminiscent of a lectern at a conference. Home territory.

"Let's talk until the police come," she said, her eyes wandering from one to another.

Though Carmen looked apprehensive, she held her peace. Separated by two yards from his captive neighbor, Doug wriggled on his chair, making Agnes fear he might topple like the trees outside.

"Mrs. Mae?" It came out like a squawk, and he cleared his throat. "Did Agnes tell—"

"Douglas Junior," cried their hostess, levering herself with outstretched arms into a shaky stand behind the table. She glared at the man. "I'm through with you! If I hadn't—"

"Er, Theresa?" Agnes interrupted. "Let me speak."

"Well, dear. There's a limit to what a body can bear," the older woman grumbled and sank back, deflated.

"Go on, then," Kieran said from across the room. One hand grabbing the rifle, he pulled out a chair at the foyer end of the long harvest table and placed the weapon on the tabletop. He straddled the chair and crossed his arms on the top rail as if settling in for a good yarn.

All eyes on her, Agnes straightened and suppressed a tremor of nerves at giving an unscripted speech.

"Doug's right about a discovery," she said. "It turns out far more complex. Let me explain. You can set me straight if I've got it wrong. Deal?"

Carmen eyed her warily while Doug bucked up. The cousins nodded encouragement. Elbows resting on the table, Theresa's hands clutched her reddened cheeks.

Agnes leaned forward to check on Joe. His jaws masticated unperturbed. "Alright by me, lass," he said when catching her eye.

Agnes fixed her glance on Carmen, saying, "It all started—at least, for me—with a balaclava. I found it on the floor between my door and the room diagonally across and looped it over that door's knob. Later, it was gone."

"Oi," said Kieran and shot a glance at Rob next to Agnes.

They must have suspected all along, Agnes realized. Why else would they come back armed?

To Carmen, she said, "You watched me, didn't you? We'd been talking moments earlier."

Carmen pouted and knotted her brows while Doug nodded approval.

Assured of her listeners' attention, Agnes continued, "When we listened to the hurricane report and newscast about the fatal robbery at the Blyte convenience store, my find took on a sinister meaning. The anchor's description of two male suspects—one a 6-footer, the other around 5'6", together with what sounded to me like 'balaclava'—triggered my alarm bells."

Agnes turned to Rob. "And then you got up and stood right next to Kieran."

"Did I?" Rob frowned. "Happens often, I guess." His frown morphed into a broad grin. "Hey. I get it. You thought me and Kieran held up the store."

"Not funny, bud," Kieran rebuked him. "The fella died."

"Sorry, man. Wasn't thinking."

Agnes intervened. "Seeing you side-by-side after hearing the description, Carmen said to me, 'About the right size.' Which confirmed my gut reaction." Focused on Kieran, Agnes explained, "You see, I believed the whole time you and Rob had the room across from mine."

"Whyever would you think that?" cut in Theresa, shaking her head. "Two men in a queen-size bed? I ask you?" She regarded Kieran as if measuring him. "Mind you, them twin beds are too short for a guy like you. The room's meant for kiddies."

"Made no difference last night, ma'am," he said. "A roof over our heads did the trick. Thanks to you."

"You're very welcome, I'm sure." Theresa beamed at him.

They certainly got more than they'd bargained for when their truck broke down, Agnes thought.

Doug's upper body strained forward, vying for her attention. "Could we stick to the point and get this over with? I told you, Agnes—"

"I'm getting there." Agnes gripped the chair's backrest harder and focused on Kieran. "Doug put me right early this morning. Once he told me the room across from mine was Carmen's, it all made sense."

"What got my room to do with it? Never got to sleep in it," Carmen interrupted.

Rob took a step forward, his face eager. "Pretty obvious, I'd say."

"I spell it out for you, Carmen," said Agnes. "First, if the balaclava belonged to someone in that room, it couldn't be the cousins'."

"Anyone can drop a hat." Though Carmen's tone was dismissive, Agnes detected a wary undertone.

"True," she agreed.

"Don't wear face covers 'til winter," Kieran said, making it sound like 'winner.'

"Yeah, sure, you'd say that," Carmen scoffed, but it lacked force.

"What mattered to me," Agnes continued, "someone in that room knocked me out when I went inside." She raised her hand to forestall interruptions. "Don't say I merely fainted in the hallway. I know for a fact that I was already inside your room, Carmen. Just reaching for something half-concealed by bedding."

Focused solely on Carmen, she saw the woman's thick lips pout in a defiant scowl.

"It was you, Carmen. You must have heard me and slipped behind the door. When you realized I was going to search your room, you whacked me over the head. Maybe you used that rubber-handled torch you'd carried earlier. After dragging me in the hallway, you left me there. Unconscious!" Agnes glared at the woman. "For all you knew, I might have died up there alone."

"Come off it. You're such a drama queen," Carmen cried. "It's what you get for snooping."

"Ah!" Doug cut in. "So you admit it!"

Carmen didn't deign to reply and merely glowered at him.

"Forensics will find my DNA and Carmen's prints on the torch," Agnes said with a firmness she didn't feel.

In surprise, she watched Carmen's expression change from worry to cunning. The eyes lit up.

"What would you do when a prowler sneaks into your room in this creepy place?" Carmen asked. "With Leo's killer on the loose? Hell. Me? I defend myself and take no prisoners."

"There is only one killer here," Doug said with authority. "And that's you!"

Chapter 27

"I'm no killer!" Carmen's shout reverberated in the room.

Agnes watched a whole gamut of emotions flicker over the woman's face before fear and hatred exploded into expletives.

The outburst ended with, "I wish we'd never come to this shithole of an island."

"Oi!" cried Kieran and Joe in unison.

"Ignorant dingbat." Kieran glared at Carmen and fell deeper into local lingo. "Took a spite to the place, ya did." His expression became sardonic. "Jail here's none too pleasant, I hear."

"Bloody oaf," Carmen growled. "What did I do to you, anyways? You just hate me."

He certainly disliked her from the start, thought Agnes. Time to interfere.

Rob beat her to it. With a grin, he told Carmen, "Don't take it personal. You're just like his older sister. Same size, same foul mouth. Puts his nose out of joint."

Must be pure warfare among the siblings, Agnes's mind commented.

"Dingbat that she is," Kieran muttered, "my sister's no crook.

Doesn't go around shootin' innocent folks, neither." He glowered fero-
ciously at Carmen. "Like you, killing that man."

Agnes's eyes widened as he reached a hand toward the table where
the rifle lay. "Kieran?" she said softly, not to draw attention to it.

The movement had a dramatic effect on Carmen, who sputtered,
"I didn't!" Her eyelids fluttered wildly. "Leo did. All his idea
anyways."

"Hah!" cried Doug. He'd been gloating over the squabble for a
while now, Agnes had noticed.

Calmly, Agnes intervened. "Why don't you tell us about it,
Carmen? I'm sure we'd all listen quietly." She shot Kieran a stern
glance, which made him rest his elbow casually on the table. Agnes
could have sworn his lips twitched.

"Yep, tell it all," said Rob.

"Okay, go ahead, Carmen," Agnes said quickly before another
spat could arise. At least Theresa and Joe kept out of things.

With a last venomous glare at Kieran, Carmen turned to Agnes.
"All I'd said, wouldn't it be a bloody laugh to grab the cash. And he
goes and tells the guy to hand it over."

"So, why shoot?" asked Rob.

For the first time, Agnes noticed sweat breaking out on Carmen's
wide forehead.

"How would I know?" was all the woman replied. She wriggled in
her blankets, perhaps uncomfortably warm now.

"I'm sure you do know," Agnes said. "Did the cashier refuse?"

"'Course he did. Yelled for us to get out. Leo pulled the gun when
the guy didn't shut up and put a hole in him. Just a little Asian guy he
was."

At that, Agnes grimaced. Leo panicking, however, sounded likely.
Yet, pushing the blame on the dead partner was all too easy.

"So, Leo shot the man?" she said to Carmen.

"Didn't I tell you? Are you deaf?" Carmen retorted.

From the sidelines came Farmer Joe's deep bass. "Tall like a
haystack that Leo, is he?"

They all stared at him uncomprehending.

He nodded sagely. "Word on Facebook's the big guy was the shooter. The wife sayed so at dinna."

"Goodness, Joe. Your internet's still working?" asked Theresa.

"Yeah, no. Not with power gone. Was nay five, dinna time," Joe said.

"That's bullshit," shouted Carmen. "No one saw us."

"The police will know for sure if there is a witness to the robbery and what they saw," Agnes said. "What I don't get, why did you come back here? If you robbed the store late morning, you'd have plenty of time to get away. You never made it to the bridge in Borden, did you?"

"'Course not," Carmen said. "That gunshot triggered Leo's astraphobia. Took forever to get him to shut up. And then he wanted to come back here." For a second, she looked genuinely puzzled. Then, rallied again. "Honest-to-God, Leo killed that man."

"She's lying!" cried Doug. "I told you she is the one and only killer here."

"Ahem. I don't think that's quite correct," said Agnes. "There are two. Carmen killed the cashier during the grab-and-run, to use her phrasing. You, Douglas Junior, killed Leo."

At that, both their detainees tried to jump to their feet. Doug's shorter legs defeated his purpose. His rocking back in the nick of time prevented him from pitching onto the plank floor face-first.

Swaddled in blankets, Carmen rose like a fury, the chair still attached to her back. Clearly intent on flooring Doug, she struggled to free herself from the covers.

"Cool it!" Kieran shouted and was on his feet. He pelted across the room.

Nimble Rob lunged in front of Doug's chair but turned to Carmen. "Sit," he commanded, like Carmen was an unruly pup.

Before Agnes could reach them, Kieran helped Carmen to sit without toppling. Her body slumped against the chair's back. Tears coursed down her broad cheeks. Agnes wasn't sure if it was anguish, anger, or frustration that burst forth in the woman's sobbing.

Agnes glanced over at Theresa, worried she might interfere and make things worse. But their hostess sat speechless, both hands cradling her face.

"He killed Leo." Carmen's voice broke. "Tried to shoot me——"

"That's slander," Doug yelled. "You have no proof."

Agnes faced their captives and focused on Doug. "Oh, yes, I do," she said softly. Then louder, "If everyone quiets down, I'll tell you."

The cousins retreated a few steps but remained on guard.

Unfazed by it all, Farmer Joe commented, "The wife's gonna be sore to miss this. Loves true crime shows, she does."

Worse than the unruliest class, Agnes thought.

"Let me finish," she said firmly. "The point is, Doug and I found a gun and a carton of ammunition in a duffle bag on Carmen's bed. Doug took the gun. To stow it away safely, he claimed."

Carmen turned on Agnes. "You let him take it. If he would of killed me, it be your fault."

So much for thanks from a woman she tried to save from being shot. Agnes sighed and said, "I doubt I could have stopped him. Anyway, the gun is safely stored now, and lab tests will reveal its story."

"None of this implicates me," Doug said. "Agnes, you and I agreed we must not let this ruthless killer escape. I did only my duty. The gun was the only way to stop this woman."

"Not as we heard it." Rob came to stand beside Doug's chair. "You threatened her with a bullet in her belly. Said you'd let her bleed to death. Didn't he? Kieran? Joe?"

"Sure did," the two men confirmed.

"See?" cried Carmen. "Four people heard you, scumbag." She spat in Doug's direction but missed. "What did I ever do to you, psycho?"

"You're out of your mind," Doug hissed back. "I've no reason for wanting to kill you. I deserve a medal for doing my citizen duty. I apprehended a fugitive killer."

"Doug had a very good reason." Agnes intervened. "At least, in *his* books. He believed Leo had told you, Carmen, that Doug is a drug dealer. He supplied Leo with Fentanyl on your first stay. When you returned yesterday, Leo asked for more. Doug refused. I suspect Doug thought it was too dangerous with us around. He feared we might recognize the symptoms, or Leo would rat on him."

"Said he was a user," Kieran muttered.

Agnes nodded. To Doug, she said, "You tried to trick me into believing Leo was asking for booze when I caught the two of you arguing upstairs. It was Fentanyl he wanted."

"Outrageous slander!" Doug yelled.

"A large bag of pills in your dirty laundry is enough evidence for the police, I dare say," Agnes remarked dryly.

"So he killed Leo to stop him squealing," Rob said.

"I did not!" Doug's face turned a spotty purple. "You can't pin that on me."

"Didn't you hear me?" Agnes asked. "It won't come out in the wash. The clothes you wore last night, stuffed into your laundry bag in the wardrobe, reek of puke. Don't take my word for it. Lab tests will prove it's Leo's."

"That's proves nothing." Doug glared. "Your clothes were wet, too." His eyes shot darts at Carmen. "Hers were soaked. She murdered her boyfriend. He was losing it, and she wanted to get rid of him. You said so yourself, Agnes."

"That's so not true," shouted Carmen.

Unperturbed, Agnes continued, "Just in case suspicion of foul play arose, you framed Carmen as successful escapee. Shoot and bury her. The hemlock's huge crater is a convenient grave."

Over Doug's vehement denial and Carmen's outrage, Agnes heaped on more.

"Carmen still wore the same clothes when I went to get her after we found Leo," Agnes said. "The sleeves were bone-dry. I touched them as she entered the bathroom. Her sweats got soaked when she held Leo in her arms."

A sobbing breath from Carmen interrupted.

"Except for those gray sweats," Agnes said, "there were no wet clothes in Carmen's room. Kieran's clothes were dry too, before he attempted CPR. Plus, the cousins had no reason to harm Leo. Nor had I." She paused for effect. "But you, Doug, had changed into pajamas and a bathrobe."

"You—You! Bitch!" Doug shrieked, spittle spewing.

A sharp volley of raps had Agnes spin around in Joe's direction. The man lumbered to his feet and made for the corridor to the side door.

"That'll be police, I bet," their hostess announced and heaved herself up.

"Stay put," Agnes said. She hastened after Joe, calling to Theresa. "I'll see to it."

The farmer opened the door just when Agnes caught up with him. He pressed his bulk against the jamb to allow her to see who came calling.

At a polite 8-feet distance stood a male and a female in dark blue uniforms with POLICE in white letters at chest height.

With a muttered, "You go back and hold the fort," Agnes squeezed by Joe and slipped outside.

Facing the cops squarely, she thought, Buckle up for a stormy ride.

Please follow me
amazon.com/author/evabernhard

Dear Reader

Dear Reader,

So nice to see you again! Did you enjoy Agnes's stormy night? Thanks so much for joining her on this adventure!

Agnes and her world are such a dear part of my life. She always surprises me with what she gets up to next.

Would you do me a special favor and recommend my books to your local library, please? Especially people with vision impairments will appreciate my large print editions. The books are also available as eBooks and in standard font paperback editions.

Of course, I greatly appreciate your kind feedback in Amazon reviews of my books.

Thanks so much for your continued support!

Warmest wishes,

Eva

Psst … Don't forget your to treat yourself

Louise Penfold Mysteries – Book 1 & 2 @
amazon.com/dp/B0FR6M4CTL?

Please follow me
amazon.com/author/evabernhard

The Perfect Gift...

Treat yourself and Loved Ones and tell your Friends about the
Agnes Taylor Mystery series

Standard Font and eBook Editions
amazon.com/dp/B099436TY2?
amazon.co.uk/dp/B099436TY2?
amazon.ca/dp/B099436TY2?

LARGE PRINT – AGNES TAYLOR MYSTERIES

amazon.com/dp/B0D8K71ZMM
amazon.ca/dp/B0D8K71ZMM
amazon.co.uk/dp/B0D8K71ZMM

My sincere thanks for your support!

Acknowledgments

Mother Nature's child, Fiona, inspired this book. My faithful dog and I spent that most memorable night in just such a place on PEI. I'm glad to say no human killer was present.

Of course, characters and events in this story are a figment of my imagination. Places are either invented or used fictitiously.

Sadly, the destruction wrought by the hurricane is all too real and still visible on the island and elsewhere in Atlantic Canada years later.

As always, my heartfelt thanks go to my long-term critique partner, author Rebecca Markus. Her feedback is always spot on, and her enthusiasm for my stories is my delight. Thanks a million, Rebecca! What would I do without you?

My critique partner, Cletus, and beta reader, Douglas (no connection to Mr. Junior of this story), provided astute and very helpful feedback. A big 'thank you' to both of you!

For years now, the online friendship of two author friends in the US sustains me. Daily emails with Regency romance author Shirley Marks are not only the greatest fun but perfect for professional discussions. She's always willing to cast her keen eye on cover designs and marketing blurbs. Thanks so much for always being there, Shirley!

My other author friend, Kristal Pawling Fox, and I exchange daily updates on our writing progress. Kristal allowed me to draw on her medical expertise to vet some points in my story. Special thanks to you, Kristal!

My sincere thanks to my trusted editor, Pam Clinton, who is always ready to hunt down punctuation errors and typos. Thanks, Pam! Though, by and large, we abide by CMOS, we take some editorial liberties and allow for poetic license, especially within the dialogs. Any linguistic, grammatical, stylistic, and typographic idiosyncrasies are solely my doing.

I dedicate this book to my family and to you, my kind reader. May you enjoy it.

www.ingramcontent.com/pod-product-compliance
Lightning Source LLC
Chambersburg PA
CBHW060359030726
47497CB00003B/787